I Want the Stars

Tom Purdom

Journey Press
www.galacticjourney.press

Vista, California
Journey Press

Journey Press
P.O. Box 1932
Vista, CA 92085
© Tom Purdom, 1964, 2020

CREDITS
Cover design: Sabrina Watts at Enchanted Ink Studio

First Printing March 2020

ISBN: 978-1-951320-04-1

Published in the United States of America

www.galacticjourney.press

For Will Jenkins of Philadelphia

Contents

Author's Foreword

I came to write this book because I'd just finished a year of grappling, unsuccessfully, with a novel about young people struggling with the problems of love and marriage, and I thought it might be fun to write a book where there was plenty of sweep and excitement with problems that could be settled by physical action—in Sturgeon's phrase, a book about "a man getting into a spaceship to go somewhere and do something." I like adventure science-fiction when it's well done—*The Dragon Masters*, for example—and I feel there's always a need for stories that will take the reader some place strange, give him a new slant on the universe, and let him engage in some vicarious violence and excitement.

But I think it has to be well done, and that means above all that it has to be believable. For one thing, if the characters are future people, then they should be different from present day people. And their social customs and politics should be different, too. I can't believe in—which means I can't enjoy—space adventures in which the characters all seem to be people just like Twentieth Century Americans from a society just like Twentieth Century America, and in which the technical details aren't well worked out.

For the benefit of those who sneer at adventure stories, I might add, that just by trying to tell an exciting story, I think I've ended up saying more about nuclear weapons, love, death, the meaning of life, and what it is to be human, than if I had sat down and tried to write about all those things.

—Thomas Purdom

Publisher's Introduction

Journey Press is excited to present Tom Purdom's *I Want the Stars* as its first novel reprint. Why, among thousands of potential titles, did we choose this one?

We at Journey Press live in the past. That is, we started out writing for Galactic Journey, a daily blog that's set exactly 55 years ago. Through the course of our journey, we've discovered hidden gems: lost classics that were out of print and hard to find for many modern readers.

When we discovered *I Want the Stars*, we were startled and pleased. Here was a story so mature, diverse, and with such scope that we knew modern readers would surely enjoy it as much as we did.

Tom set out to portray something unique in *I Want the Stars*. He wasn't interested in yet another space opera or translated Western, or even the projection of mid-Century Americans on the far future. You will not find 20th or 21st Century humans in this story — the headstrong protagonist Jenorden, gentle Veneleo, haunted Thelia, resourceful Elinee, are at once relatable yet different. There is no distinction or inequality between men and women, and there is a strong suggestion of polyamory amongst the crew (or at least flexible relationships without jealousy). Indeed, the book is unusually progressive even today, when gender roles are still somewhat ascendant, and "traditional marriage" is held up by many as the favored model. And yet, despite the differences, the characters and the universe Tom created are eminently compelling, relatable, and inspiring.

Which brings us to the most important reason we chose this book. *I Want the Stars* is a timeless story. More importantly, it's a story of hope. Much of science fiction is cautionary in nature: "If this goes on, bad things will happen." Less common are the aspirational stories that say, "Herein, see a world worth striving for." And given the crises we've lived through recently, such stories are needed now more than ever.

We loved the message of *I Want the Stars*. We think you will, too.

A final note: The names of two alien races in the book, "Horta" and "Borg", may ring a bell, especially if you're familiar with *Star Trek* (another space spectacular with an overriding theme of hope). It's worth keeping in mind that *I Want the Stars* was published in 1964 — two years before Star Trek made its debut! There's probably no connection...

Chapter 1

Rocketing at twice the speed of sound, holding a course so close to the water the spray misted its windows, the winged orbit-to-ground vehicle shot across the oceans of a world sixty thousand light years from Earth. Dangerous, unpredictable mountains of water rose and fell beneath the vehicle's hull, but the woman in the pilot's seat flew without looking at the waves or the controls. Her dark, serious eyes were locked on the horizon. The battle would begin the instant she saw the Horta ship.

Behind the pilot two women and a man sat in the reclining chairs of the passenger cabin. The women had been gazing at each other since the vehicle entered the atmosphere; now, knowing the battle could begin any moment, they settled back in their chairs and watched the horizon over the pilot's shoulder. The man, Jenorden A'Ley went on staring at the ocean through the misted window by his seat. There were no continents on this world, only a few hundred islands, and the waves were titanic.

He was a slight, dark man with silver hair and sharp features. Even as he rode into danger he was brooding about the passion which had sent him to the stars and which was now driving him toward the island of the Horta. It was a passion as titanic as the waves, it dominated his life and could be driving him to his death, and yet he had never found the words to describe it. In a time when linguistics and psychology were so advanced the members of the human community could communicate their thoughts and feelings with almost no distortion, no one he knew quite understood what he wanted.

"There it is!"

The woman's voice ended his reverie. His hands tightened on the arm rests. Through the front window he saw the tall Horta ship and the edge of the island. Now he was undoubtedly in range of whatever weapons the Horta possessed.

The pilot pressed a button on the control panel. Somewhere in the vehicle, a circuit closed. The mass-energy converter, which had been turning water into energy and using the energy to propel the vehicle, now sent a fraction of its energy flowing toward the cannon in the nose. High explosive shells screamed toward the island.

The Horta ship grew taller and blacker, rising out of the ocean until it towered above the mosquito darting toward it across the waves. He could see the gun turrets, and the crude seams in the metal, and the one porthole in the nose. They skimmed over the breakers and he saw white shapes running across the beach. Once every half second a shell screamed out of the cannon. Veering away from their target, they soared across the island. The vehicle banked and the ground dropped away and for a brief instant he saw the wall which cut the island in half, on one side the flat beach the Horta used for a landing site, on the other side the stone buildings they had erected with the labor of their slaves. Then he was shooting across the waves again, fleeing toward the horizon, and Roseka was leaning out of her chair and staring through the rear window.

"Make another run!" Roseka shouted.

"Did I get it?" Elinee asked.

"No."

"I was aiming right at it."

"You were hitting to the left," Jenorden said.

Elinee swung them into a wide turn. They all knew they had to strike fast, before the Horta could ready their weapons or get their ship off the ground. The ship looked primitive, but they were certain it was better armed than their vehicle. If the Horta ever got off the ground, they would have to give up and run for space.

"Is everybody all right?" Elinee asked.

Roseka turned to Thelia My, the woman sitting beside her, and they regarded each other gravely. "We're doing very well," Thelia said.

For a moment he envied them. Roseka and Thelia were lovers and had been ever since the last decade of their schooling. Everything they experienced, their thoughts, their work, their affairs with men, every love and hate and pleasure, was shared and communicated. They had created a psychological relationship which impressed everyone who knew them. He had never felt the need for such a relationship, but now, conscious he was riding toward the Horta guns—and this time the Horta were prepared—he knew he was more alone than any human should be.

The raid had been Roseka's idea. She had been determined to contact the Horta since the moment the changing colors on the Sordini's forehead had first told them what the Horta were.

"They do things to your mind," the Sordini said. "Once they've had time to work on you, you do what they want."

"Telepaths!" Veneleo whispered.

Roseka gasped. She was a psychologist and no group of humans had ever encountered a telepathic race. Most psychologists had come to believe telepathy was impossible. In all the records of all the thousands of races mankind had contacted, there was no evidence that any being in the galaxy had ever encountered a telepath.

"What do they do?" Roseka asked. "What do they do to your mind?"

Veneleo bent over his machine and tapped out her question on the keyboard. On top of the machine a yellow and green light flickered and changed shade while the Sordini watched it intently. The Sordini were amphibians who spent most of their time under water and communicated by modulating the color of a fleshy organ in their forehead. Veneleo had established communication with them by first teaching them a simple color language which had been developed by the contact experts of the human community; once the amphibians had learned the simple language, it had taken him less than a day to learn the Sordini language.

"We don't know what they do," the Sordini signaled. "Some of us have felt their touch and escaped, but no one has felt them long enough to learn what they do."

"How long does it take them?" Roseka asked.

"We think it takes several minutes."

"Are they spreading their influence?" Jenorden asked.

"Yes. We try to fight them, but they send our own people against us. Until you came, it was hopeless."

"Macrella's theory," Roseka said.

"Which theory is Macrella's?" Jenorden asked.

"Macrella thought telepathy would tend to cause paranoia. If it were a mutation, if some race acquired it suddenly, after they'd always been able to think and feel in private, Macrella demonstrated the most likely reaction was hate. The telepath would have other people's emotions pouring into his psyche and most of the emotions would be repulsive to him. In many cases they'd be emotions the telepath had driven into his unconscious. He'd have to try to make the other mind repress them, too. A telepath would probably have a compulsion to dominate every mind around him, to make every mind have feelings he could tolerate."

"That could even drive them off their own world," Jenorden said. "They couldn't live with each other."

"Possibly. It sounds logical."

"It sounds terrible," Elinee said.

"It's the most exciting thing we've run into," Roseka said. "This could revolutionize every culture in the galaxy. The Horta have a tool which could solve every psychological mystery."

Veneleo smiled. "All we have to do is talk them into cooperating."

Jenorden pointed at the Sordini. The amphibian's forehead was pulsing like a beacon.

"What's he saying?" Roseka asked.

Veneleo studied the swiftly changing colors. The message went on for a long time. "He wants us to help them. He's asking us to fight the Horta. He thinks we've got the equipment to do it."

"You sound like you think we don't," Roseka said.

"You know what kind of weapons we've got. Even if they weren't telepaths, it would be foolish. We're armed for self-defense."

"I'm thinking about hitting them fast and taking one prisoner. We could study it and we might learn how to reach them. They're insane but that doesn't mean they're beyond help."

"What makes you think we can get that close without becoming slaves?"

"He said it takes them a few minutes to get control. If we hit them by surprise and work fast, we may be able to do it."

"And what if we fail?"

"I'm willing to take the risk."

"I'm not."

"Then don't do it. I'm suggesting it so everyone can think about it. Maybe the others are interested."

"What will we do with a prisoner if we get one?" Jenorden asked. "How do you think we can keep him from working on us?"

"We can put him in a robot vehicle and send him out past the fifth planet. We'll keep a few million miles between our ship and the vehicle and I'll study him a few minutes at a time."

"You'll be taking some terrible risks, Roseka."

"I know it's dangerous. I wouldn't do it for anything that wasn't this important."

"They're destroying the Sordini," Elinee said. "They're enslaving an entire race. We should do something."

"It's none of our business," Veneleo said. "You'll get killed for nothing."

"It's nothing to you," Roseka said, "but that doesn't mean it's nothing to everybody else."

They returned to their star ship and made a reconnaissance from orbit, and the argument went on. Veneleo was definitely against it and Thelia would go wherever Roseka went, but Elinee and Jenorden couldn't make up their minds. And Roseka felt she needed four people, three to make the landing and one to pilot the vehicle.

Jenorden was tempted. He would have said yes right away if he hadn't been afraid. When he lay with Roseka that night, they spent hours discussing his emotions and only a few minutes enjoying their bodies. He was afraid to die, and he was afraid of what the Horta could do to his mind, but he was driven by a need to experience everything a human being could experience.

He had grown up in a time when war was as obsolete as sickness and poverty. It had been almost a century since men had last pointed weapons at their own kind. He was glad of that, every member of the human community considered it mankind's greatest victory, and yet he knew he had missed an experience which had once been a common part of human life. Men had been warriors since they first inhabited the Earth. How could he feel he had known the full range of human experience if he lived out his three centuries without once going into battle?

He would probably never have another chance like this one. Humans never had to fight advanced races, and if they were attacked on primitive worlds they retreated as fast as they could. Here, uniquely, was a situation in which attack could be morally justified. The passion which had sent him to the stars was now demanding he go with Roseka against the Horta.

All through his education, the forty-seven years when everything you did was planned by the community so you would grow to full human stature, he had been obsessed with the size of the universe. He had grown up knowing the galaxy was inhabited by thousands of races, each one unique and with a history and culture as complicated as the history and culture of mankind. Every year since his twelfth birthday ships had returned from the stars with news of inhabited worlds. Life flowered everywhere. A man could live a million centuries and never know it all.

He had roamed the stars for eight years now and he knew his hunger could never be satisfied. He couldn't forget all the places he had never seen, and the knowledge he hadn't learned, and the intelligent beings he had never met. He wanted to experience the whole universe, every star, every life, every world, and the knowledge that it was impossible tormented every hour of his days. He could cross the Milky Way in months and yet, when he compared the limits of his mortal consciousness to the infinite size of the universe, he felt as confined and as angry as a prisoner in a six foot square cell.

He had to have this. He had to know how combat felt. It was part of life and he didn't want to miss anything.

Elinee was just as tormented. He slept with her the next night and once again he spent most of the time talking. Her needs were very similar to his. She, too, wanted to experience everything. She had come on this voyage because she thought she was an artist. She thought there was some work growing in her imagination and she was feeding whatever it was with everything she experienced. Someday, if she was an artist, it would bloom. She was a human being and this was the first century of the first human civilization. No member of the human community had to work or do anything else he didn't want to do. Every member of the human community could have anything he wanted, including a ship which could cross the galaxy in months, simply by asking for it. She could do as she pleased with three centuries of life.

"I'm not just afraid of death, Jenorden. I'm afraid this will do something to me."

"We have to decide something. We've been thinking about this for two days now. We haven't had a good moment since we got here."

"I know. Even Veneleo's getting moody."

"I don't feel like I'm deciding something. I feel like I'm trying to accept my fate. I know what I'm going to do. All I'm doing now is hesitating."

"Then let's wake them up and tell them we're going to do it."

He stiffened. "You've decided?"

"I'm as decided as I'll ever be."

They woke up the others. As he had expected, the news didn't start a celebration. Veneleo looked stunned. Roseka nodded soberly and suggested they make the attack right after breakfast.

Elinee was still undecided. Speeding toward the island, making their second attack, Jenorden saw the tracers passing to the right of the ship and he knew her lack of skill wasn't the only reason she was missing. Even an inexperienced gunner should be able to put at least one shell on a target that big. They veered to the right and he cringed when he heard bullets clanging on the vehicle's armor.

"What's wrong?" Roseka demanded. "What are you doing, Elinee?"

Elinee didn't answer. The horizon came between them and the ship and she banked into another turn. In a moment they would be heading back toward the island.

Jenorden unbuckled his seat belt, and made his way to the front of the cabin. By now the Horta probably had their big guns ready.

"Let me take it, Elinee."

"I'll hit it this time."

"You don't want to hit it."

She had answered him without looking up. Now she raised her head, and her eyes looked so tortured they pleaded with him. Humans could hide very little from themselves. Repressed desire, the cause of so much mental illness, was almost a thing of the past. One sentence from another human had made her accept the truth she had been evading.

"This will be our last chance," he said. "It isn't your fault you aren't a destroyer."

She turned them away from the island. Switching on the robot pilot, she slid out of her seat.

He sat down and strapped himself in. As soon as Elinee was safe in a passenger seat, he turned toward the island. The ship appeared on the horizon and something wild leaped in his psyche. The vehicle fitted him like a shell. The cannon was a natural extension of his mind. Mankind had abolished war, and he could roam the stars as a member of an advanced race, but at that moment he knew men were still barbarians. His hand tightened on the wheel.

Three puffs of smoke appeared on the ship's back sides. He cringed, but this time his fear drove him forward. His thumb pressed the trigger button and a shell screamed out of the cannon.

A Horta shell exploded on his right. The wheel fought his hands as the sudden pressure on the right wing made the vehicle bank. His arm muscles strained and he felt the vehicle turn left and climb. For a moment he saw the sun and a big yellow cloud. He turned his head and spied the ship over the leading edge of the right wing. Far below, a tracer bullet shot across the waves.

He rolled out of the climb. Pressing the trigger button in until it locked, he drove toward the ship. The cannon growled rhythmically. More puffs appeared on the ship's side. He couldn't see the ammunition speeding toward him, but he knew it was there and he knew what it could do to him. Clenching his teeth, taking pride in the strength of his will, he held the vehicle on a long incline which ended in the middle of the ship's hull. The barbarian was all the way out now. He was enjoying this.

A shell rammed the base of the ship and exploded. The ship rocked and a ring of smoke surrounded its tail. He veered away from his target, banked, and dove again. The first shell out of the cannon exploded just above the ship's middle. A second explosion went off next to the first and then a series of explosions hammered the entire vessel. The ship tilted and began to fall. He climbed and dove again, this time on a wrecked, toppling hull, and two more explosions sent the Horta vessel crashing to the beach.

He circled the island, inspecting the wreckage. The nose dropped and he dove again. Coming in low over the beach, he sent two shells screaming toward the wall and climbed above the stone buildings. When he looked back, he saw smoke drifting away from a breach in the wall. He climbed to twenty-thousand feet, leveled off, and turned on the robot pilot.

Elinee came forward and took his place. He felt exhausted. As he returned to his seat, all his taut muscles and nerves suddenly relaxed. He became aware of an ache in his jaw and he realized he had been clenching his teeth ever since he took over the pilot's seat.

They came in over the breakers and made a smooth landing on the beach. Elinee turned the vehicle until the cannon pointed at the breach in the wall.

Jenorden and the other two women stood up and started putting on their equipment. They were all wearing the light, transparent pressure suits humans wore on alien planets at all times; pulling the rolled collars over their heads, they zipped themselves in. From a rack in the rear of the cabin, they each took a mass-energy converter and a pistol and holster.

Elinee started the airlock cycle. The inner door opened and they entered the lock and waited for the signal to open the outer door. Jenorden drew his pistol and Roseka and Thelia unsnapped their holsters.

They lived in the dawn of human freedom. Masters of the star drive, citizens of a world community so wealthy it could satisfy every material desire without human labor, men went where they wanted and did what they pleased. They followed their hearts and nothing else. Waiting for the signal, he stared at his gun and wondered why he should have the bad luck to be the slave of a heart which needed more than life could possibly give it, a heart which drove him from folly to folly.

The outer door glowed. He opened it and one by one they went down the ladder to the beach.

Chapter 2

They spread out and started walking toward the wall with drawn guns. The waves thundered on the beach and the ocean and the sky seemed immense.

Elinee turned the vehicle around and took off over the ocean. She would circle at thirty-thousand feet and return when they called her.

They were beautiful people and they walked with the grace of creatures who have perfect control of their bodies. There were no awkward, ugly humans anymore. Roseka was blonde and voluptuous, with a rolling stride which made men feel with their eyes the soft flesh of her body, and Thelia was a slender girl with long black hair and an oval face. They would be as youthful and healthy as they were now until the moment they died.

"You really messed things up," Roseka said. "They should be stunned."

Jenorden kept his left hand near his belt. The third button on the left activated a force shield which repelled all missiles weighing less than six ounces and moving at less than eighteen hundred feet per second. The shield had to be used sparingly, only when needed, because it used up so much energy the converter on his back could only keep it activated for a few minutes.

Their pistols used the same mechanism as the cannon on the nose of their vehicle. A unit of energy from the converter moved a piston which propelled the bullet. Various weapons had been designed for self-defense on alien worlds and this system had proved to be the best. Radiation weapons were too dangerous to the user, and weapons which used an explosion to propel a bullet were hard to adapt to atmospheres with varying percentages of oxygen. The system was ideal for self-defense, which was all it had been designed for, but Jenorden knew they would probably be outgunned when they clashed with the Horta.

The ocean and the beach reminded him of all the pleasures he had enjoyed on Earth. If this were Earth, he could take off his suit and feel the air and the sun on his flesh. He could even bathe in the ocean. Earth was a garden. Every place on it was a source of pleasure. There were forests and mountains and pretty little places where you drank wine next to carefully arranged scenery. He had gone on parties which lasted for weeks and which circled the world several times, dining at the North Pole, singing and playing instruments in African jungles, dancing on top of Mount Everest, riding camels over deserts…

For eight years he had spent every minute of his life in the artificial atmosphere of a suit or the artificial atmosphere of the ship. For eight years he had lived without the tang and variety of natural air, air which could be hot and cold, dense and thin, and without the water of the ocean, and rain, and without those wonderful days when two and three hundred thousand members of his species gathered in one place for the joy of being human together. He had been separated from everything he loved, and now he was risking all of it for an experience men had once tried to avoid.

"What are you feeling?" Roseka asked. "Do you notice anything strange?"

"I'm thinking about Earth," Jenorden said. "I think I'm getting homesick."

"How about you, Thelia?"

"Just apprehension. I expected that. What are you feeling?"

"I feel very calm. I haven't felt this calm in months. I think you'd better watch me, both of you. I don't like it. Are you still thinking about Earth, Jenorden?"

"We've been away a long time, haven't we? If we die, we'll never…"

He stopped. He choked and then he threw up his hands as if he were warding off a blow.

"What's the matter?" Roseka said. "Keep talking. Keep talking."

He was looking at the universe. He was standing on the edge of space and the galaxies were turning before him. The whole vast panorama had suddenly appeared in his mind. Stars burst into flame and flickered out. Millions of intelligent life forms struggled to survive, built star ships, wandered and fought and created, and died, and were as if they had never existed. It was more than consciousness could bear. He cringed in terror. Before the juggernaut, the universe rolling through time, he was nothing. His entire life would only be an instant. Already the cold was creeping through his veins.

"What is it, Jenorden?"

He couldn't answer. His arms dangled at his sides, the gun completely forgotten. He had seen this vision before, but never so intensely. He knew what it meant to be mortal. He was moving toward death, and death negated everything an intelligent being could achieve. He was dying. Everything was dying. He had been dying since the moment he took root in the womb.

A white head rose above the wall. Roseka screamed and both women turned on the white, strangely formless shape and brought their pistols up to eye level. Hate twisted their faces.

Activating his shield, he stood there and watched them shoot. Three more shapes appeared at the far end of the wall and he watched as they aimed their rifles. He knew he should protect the women, who were still firing at the lone Horta in front of them, but he was paralyzed by the vision of his own futility. He felt as if he were already dead. He was a stiff, ghostly spectator at a drama which had no effect on his emotions.

Three Horta rifles cracked at once. Thelia spun and her pistol flew from her hand and dangled from the wires which attached it to her converter. He watched her crumple, the first violent death he had ever witnessed, and his shoulders drooped.

Roseka screamed and turned on the three Horta without activating her shield. She was outgunned but she was trying to fight without protecting herself. She had to die sometime. *Life is painful. Death is the absence of pain. Death is just like sleep.*

He felt the alien mind flicker in his consciousness and he understood what was happening. The Horta had found his weakness seconds after he landed on the island. They had detected his underlying sense of futility and they were using it to paralyze him.

He stared at Thelia's body. *That is death. That is what you are becom-*

ing. That is the goal of your life.

The Horta were the loveliest music he had ever heard. They sang to him from the deepest regions of his psyche. He felt as peaceful and sleepy as he had the month he had slept every night in a yacht in the middle of the South Atlantic. He closed his eyes and yawned.

More Horta appeared on the wall. Roseka turned on them, screaming every time she fired, and they all took aim. She still didn't have her shield on.

Two Horta slid behind the wall with mangled heads. The carnage was disgusting. Roseka was a killer, too. They were only defending themselves and look what she was doing to them. She had come here to capture an intelligent being and experiment with it as if it were some kind of laboratory animal. This was an immoral, foolish expedition and she had talked them into it. She deserved to die.

His muscles quivered as if they were struggling against chains. The Horta had found his weakness. His personality had been shaped by forty-seven years of education designed to create a conscience which would make him fit to control the immense powers of his species. In spite of everything they were doing to him, a segment of his personality knew he couldn't let another human being die. They had hit him by surprise, before he even knew he was being attacked, but now that tiny, warring segment was trying to marshal psychological forces which would liberate him from the Horta.

Visions of the pleasant world of Earth floated in his consciousness. He swam and danced and hiked. He kissed a slender young redhead—he was only seventeen—in the lovely waterfront streets of a city where great unmanned ships came up the river from the ocean. He listened to a hundred thousand voices sing a hymn to Earth composed by a great musician who had been a founder of the human community. Memories crowded through his skull until he was so enraptured he could hardly see the battle going on in front of him.

A bullet kicked up the dust at Roseka's feet. The Horta were bad shots but they exposed themselves to Roseka's fire as if they didn't know what death was.

They're undefeatable. They can't be beaten.

Again he detected an alien thought. They were using every psychological persuasion possible—you can't win, the enemy is undefeatable, your side is in the wrong, the fight isn't worth it, go home and have a good time.

Earth sang in his brain. He knew what they were doing, but the knowledge wasn't enough. He was still chained. He still didn't have the weapon to fight them. Perhaps there wasn't any weapon. Perhaps he should lie on the sand and enjoy his dying moments dreaming about Earth. The Horta couldn't be fought. Roseka was going to die, and after that his shield would use up all the energy in his converter, and he would lie there unprotected while the Horta filled him with bullets. If he died with his brain full of dreams, he wouldn't even know they were killing him.

He would never see his own lovely world. He would never breathe natural air. He would never again experience the happiness of living in unity with the members of his own race.

The sudden attack jolted him so hard he doubled over. The rush of emotion nauseated him. The unconquered, struggling portion of his ego had seized its first opportunity. The Horta had been using his memories of Earth to paralyze him with a longing which made him unable to risk his life. Now that little piece of human will took his natural desire to live and used the memories evoked by the Horta to intensify it. Two sets of emotions clashed in his psyche.

He opened his mouth and one foot shuffled forward. Leaning into a frozen half step, he stood there and strangled on what he wanted to say.

"Elinee... land."

His radio was on and his mike was attached to his throat. His voice sounded strange and choked, but he knew she could hear him.

"Ro... se... ka..."

A bullet knocked Roseka's legs out from under her. She screamed and fell on her face and as soon as she hit the sand she raised her head and started shooting. Her anger was stronger than her pain. Two Horta fell away from the wall without a sound of pain.

Her suit had automatically sealed the bullet hole, protecting her from alien bacteria, but he could see the blood spurting from her wound. The bullet had punctured an artery. Even if they didn't wound her again, she would bleed to death in a few minutes.

He stared at her wound. The Horta visions were powerful and

confusing. Only by looking at her blood could he remain aware she was hurt and dying and needed his help.

He was on Earth. He was home. He was standing on a beach and a girl was waiting for him in the breakers. When he entered the water, he would taste the salt on his bare lips.

A fountain of blood spurted through his vision. He stared at the blood, at the wound, at another member of his own species, and he took a full step forward. A bullet cracked on his shield. He moved clumsily, like some monster created by a blundering genetics engineer. He had to fight his own emotions all the way. He wanted to look at the sky and the ocean — this is Earth, lie down, lie down — but he had to look at her wound. He would bleed like that, too. Her blood and his blood were the same color and the same chemistry. When they shot their final volley, he would bleed like that from half a dozen holes at once.

He stopped. It was like walking in a three-g gravity field. His legs felt numb. He wanted to lie down and rest and let the Horta sing him to his death. Staring at Roseka's wound, he raised his hand and yawned. He couldn't move.

He gathered what little drive he had. Dropping to his knees, he threw himself forward.

His hand found her waist. When he raised his eyes, she was still screaming and shooting. He pushed in the button and a bullet ricocheted off her shield.

Something was roaring in the sky. He twisted his head and saw Elinee skim across the waves and land on the beach.

"Look... out... get us off..."

"What's wrong, Jenorden?"

"In... our mind... careful..."

"Can you walk to the airlock?"

"Roseka... shot..."

"Thelia! Is Thelia dead?"

"...ahhhhh..."

"Hold on!"

Her voice cracked. As the vehicle rolled up the beach, the sobs in his earphones were louder than the roar of the engines.

Waves of apathy and bleakness rolled through his mind. Life was pain without a purpose. He was tired of feeling. Emotion was a torment. He could sink, he was sinking, into a peace as soft and gentle as the ocean. This is the peace of the Horta. Take the gift of the Horta.

The vehicle stopped between him and the wall. "Can you move her?" Elinee asked.

"Help... me...."

"Why did we do this? Roseka, what are you doing?"

Roseka was shooting at the Horta through the space between the sand and the bottom of the vehicle. She had stopped screaming, but the muscles of her face were frozen in the same expression of intense hate they had assumed when the Horta first appeared on the wall. Jenorden pushed her waist, unlocking his paralysis that much, and suddenly she wiggled forward, under the vehicle, and crawled toward the wall.

"Stop her, Jenorden!"

"...peace..."

"I can feel them!"

Blackness was creeping through his bones. His legs were growing stiff. He could feel the cells of his brain shutting off. It was like falling asleep. He knew Roseka had been shooting so much her shield was almost ready to collapse, leaving her unarmed and unprotected, but he could hardly keep his eyes open.

A spasm shook his entire body. His fingers clawed the sand. He looked at Thelia's body and he knew what it meant to die.

The Horta had gone too far. They had brought him so close to death even his numbed, exhausted mind had to feel the terror of nonexistence. At the edge of extinction, he recoiled.

He put his hands under his shoulders and lifted himself to his knees. His muscles trembled as he pushed against the weight of his despair. A hail of bullets rattled on his shield. The Horta struggled to retain control, but they had provoked an emotion so powerful it couldn't be restrained. He stared at Roseka with the dumb, brutal eyes of an intelligent being who has lost every feeling but the need to live.

"Jenorden, they're inside my mind!"

He grunted. One human urge remained from all those years of education. He couldn't leave Roseka. She was human.

He stood up and shuffled around the vehicle. The Horta could still slow him down, but they had aroused something so basic it would take them a long time to dominate it. He didn't want to be dead like Thelia. He would kill every living thing on this planet before he would let them kill him.

Roseka's shield collapsed just before he stepped in front of her. Putting his foot on her hand, he crushed her fingers until she released the gun. She looked up, snarling like an animal, and he bent down and grabbed her shoulders.

"Kill them! Kill them! Kill them!"

He hit her in the jaw with the edge of his palm. Keeping his shield between her and the Horta rifles, he picked her up and carried her toward the vehicle. The bone had cut through her leg but the important thing right now was speed. The ship's hospital could repair any damage he was doing. Already he could feel the Horta eroding his drive. They had discovered the sensitive human was revolted by this upsurge of the animal, and they were bringing the sensitive human back to power. They could be surprised, but they weren't stupid.

"Open the airlock, Elinee!"

"They're getting me."

"*Open it!*"

He had never heard a human voice growl like that. The sound would have terrified him if he hadn't been driven by the animal need which produced it.

The airlock opened. He lifted Roseka and shoved her through the door. The ladder came up and he went up it in one motion, pushing the button which closed the door at the same time he stepped over Roseka.

"Go!"

"I can't," Elinee moaned.

The outer door closed behind him and he immediately pushed the button which unlocked the inner door. He didn't have time to unsuit and go through the sterilizing process. The cabin was already infected with something worse than disease.

Elinee was staring out the front window. She was humming to herself and her fingers were scratching the control panel.

She didn't resist him when he unstrapped her and pulled her out of the seat. He pushed her into a passenger chair, fastening the belt for her, and she stared at him with eyes which reflected the struggle going on in her mind.

He slid behind the controls. The Horta were singing about Earth again. He was leaving Earth, not an island on a planet sixty-thousand light years from Earth. He was leaving peace and fresh air and forests where people could hike for weeks in perfect solitude.

He fastened his seat belt and turned the vehicle toward the ocean. When the landing gear finally left the beach, he was crying.

Chapter 3

He turned on the robot pilot and returned to the airlock. Roseka was moaning in pain. She had recovered from whatever madness the Horta had given her, but she was still incoherent. He gave her first aid, applying a tourniquet and splinting her leg, and shot an anaesthetic drug into her thigh.

When they reached the star ship, he and Veneleo put her in the hospital and the hospital immediately sent her into therapeutic shock and began repairing the damage. In a few days her body would be exactly as it had been. Everywhere the members of the human community traveled, the best of their medical techniques traveled with them.

Healing the mind was a different matter. As soon as Roseka was settled in the hospital, the three who were physically unharmed retired to their quarters.

Jenorden felt drained of all emotion. When he slumped into his arm chair, he pressed the emergency therapy button only because he had been trained to, not because he cared what happened to him.

"What happened?" a voice asked.

"We landed on the island."

"Why?"

"How should I know?"

A moment passed while his answer was analyzed by the computer which occupied half the ship's volume. Impulses flowed along circuits, choices were made according to a program designed by the best therapists in the community, and again the voice asked a question.

"Why do you think you don't know?"

Something hissed in a comer of the room. Sniffing the air, he realized the computer had released a psycho-active gas. He must sound pretty recalcitrant. It didn't matter. He was too tired to care.

His limbs relaxed. He closed his eyes and for the next hour the computer asked him questions which made him examine his emotions. The process wasn't as efficient as analysis with a human therapist, but Roseka wasn't available, and in the end it did the same job. The goal was complete self-awareness. All repressed emotions had to be brought to consciousness. Every human subjected his emotions to this kind of objective questioning at least once a week.

"Is this helping?" the machine asked.

"Some. It can't help much."

"Why not?"

"I'm not hiding from anything. I can't. I want to but I can't. I've seen what death is. This is what I've been fighting all my life and now it's more real than it's ever been. Therapy can keep me from running away from it, but it can't tell me what the answer is."

"No more questions."

He sat there a few minutes longer and then he got up and took his musical instrument off the wall. That session had been necessary for his health, but it had added nothing to his happiness. Someday, somewhere in the universe, before his despair paralyzed him and turned him into a walking dead man, he had to find an answer to what the Horta had taught him. As he carried his instrument to the common area, he felt the heavy weight on his shoulders, and the weariness in his limbs, and he knew that moment of living death was only a few years away.

Music was as much a part of human communication as speech. Every human played at least one instrument, and most played several. He played only one, the third instrument in the modern violin family, an instrument with a range higher than the old violoncello, but lower than the old viola. He had fallen in love with its somber, lyrical voice when he was a boy of eleven, and fifty years of playing had only made him love it more.

When he reached the common, Veneleo and Elinee were already playing a duet. Behind them, as the ship accelerated away from the sun, the stars were marching across a tall window. They were both playing the second instrument in the violin family, a significant choice for Veneleo, who usually played the flute or the trumpet.

He sat down. Veneleo and Elinee had begun a coda and were working their way toward a climax. They were good improvisers, and he wasn't, so they usually let him choose the basic piece. He waited until the duet faded out in a climax of understated grief, and then he began a long, quiet solo from a sonata a friend of his had written many years before, when they were both hopelessly in love with a great beauty. The music used all the power of the instrument's middle range, and he played it with the passion of an artist who has such control of his medium he can forget his hands and his tools and let his emotions run wild.

There were no words. There never would be words. Thelia was dead. Roseka was hurt. Jenorden had seen too much.

The ship accelerated beyond the speed of light. Shutters automatically slid across the windows, blocking out the strange, milky whiteness few humans could tolerate for long. Hours passed as they streaked across the light years toward a new sun. Inside the ship, the music shook and groaned and soared. Jenorden played as if he wanted to fill the universe with sound.

They approached a star four light years from the system they had just left and the ship decelerated below the speed of light. Taking over the controls, Veneleo put them in an orbit around the new star, and told the computer to open the dome over the common.

The shutters slid back. Sunlight exactly like the sunlight of home flooded the big room. The ship was now a small planet in an orbit calculated to give them the same heat and light they would have enjoyed on Earth.

Elinee arranged some furniture around the pool and Veneleo and Jenorden brought trees and flowers from the hydroponics farm. None of them said much. They all knew what they needed. They lay in the sun, and they napped, they swam, and whenever their feelings got too painful for comfort, they picked up their instruments and turned their grief into music.

Roseka returned to consciousness on the second day. The hospital let them visit her for half an hour. When she asked about Thelia, they all hesitated. She burst into sobs before they could tell her, and the hospital immediately put her to sleep.

The hospital kept her unconscious for three more days. The next time they saw her, she was standing in the door of the common room. She started to talk, and then she shook her head and ran to her quarters.

That night, and for the next week, she slept with Veneleo. She had always insisted they change sex partners frequently, to avoid the troubles caused by strong attachments in a small group, but they all knew Veneleo was the kind of man she needed at this moment. Veneleo was gay and comforting and sympathetic. Jenorden gave women pleasure and excitement, but he had never yet given one rest.

Soon there were four of them lounging around the swimming pool. For once even Jenorden didn't want to move on. Another week passed before he and Roseka discussed what had happened on the island.

As he had guessed, the Horta had simply aroused her hatred. She was very ashamed of this. She had made love the central theme of her life, and she had trouble, though it was necessary therapy, admitting she was a person with many strong dislikes.

"They went right into me," she said. "They flooded me with hate. I wanted to kill them so bad I couldn't think."

"I didn't think they'd be so fast," Jenorden said.

"They found your weakness and mine in less than a minute."

"I think they did some permanent damage, Roseka."

"It's too early to tell."

"Don't you think they did something permanent to you?"

"Please."

"You have to talk about it. You may as well talk about it with somebody who was there."

She was responsible for their psychic health, but they were all collectively responsible for hers. Now she did something he had seen her do before when he was acting as her therapist and she had to say something difficult; she looked at a point in space just above his shoulder and then she threw her head back and looked him in the eye.

"I can't give up," she said. "I have to reach the Horta. I can't let Thelia die for nothing."

"Do you still think it's possible?"

"I have to try."

He put his hand on her shoulder. He wanted to comfort her, but he didn't know how to do it.

"If you ever go back there, Roseka, I'll have to go with you."

"If I could leave them alone, I'd do it. I'm not sure the human race has evolved to a point where we can face what they make us face."

"Do you have any idea how it can be done?"

She shook her head. "It's obvious we can't do it by force. Even if we'd taken one prisoner, I think they showed us we couldn't have handled him. We have to learn how to open our minds to them without being manipulated." The words flowed out of her mouth. She had obviously been giving this a lot of thought. "We have to learn how to manipulate them. That won't be easy, either. This will take the best we've got. I'm going to go on educating myself, traveling and learning just as I have been, and when we get home, I'll set up a research project. Every advanced race in the galaxy should be interested in this. With all that intellect to draw on, we should be able to find a way."

She had found her career. His own sanity, and everything that mattered to him of his life, could depend on her success.

More days drifted by. Little by little he felt his restlessness returning. It wasn't as sharp as it had been before he met the Horta, but he found himself pacing the edge of the pool and thinking about all the unexplored stars he could see through the windows.

"Jenorden's ready to go," Elinee said.

"How can you tell?" Veneleo asked.

He took off his shirt and dove into the pool. He was too tense to engage in banter. He swam the length of the pool four times, trying to use up his extra energy, and then he climbed out and stretched himself on a reclining chair. Five minutes after he sat down, he was pacing the deck again.

"I think we're ready to move," Veneleo said. He strolled across the common to the control room.

A few minutes later the shutters slid across the dome. Veneleo returned to the pool and dove in without a word. No one bothered to ask where they were going. They swam, and then ate lunch, and all the while the giant, battered sphere accelerated past the speed of light and sped toward the nearest star.

They were in a cluster no human had ever explored. Men had

been wandering the stars for over fifty years, and the libraries of Earth had tapes describing the language and customs and history of thousands of worlds, but there were still immense regions of the galaxy which had never been visited by man or by any race known to man. They had come here because eight years of visiting planets already known to the human community had bored them with being mere tourists. This was far more exciting. They were surrounded by mystery. Anything could be waiting for them out there.

The first system they entered was a double star. As they had expected, it had no planets. They moved on, crossing five more light years, and entered a system with two planets, one of them a giant and one about half the size of Earth. On the smaller planet they found the remains of a civilization which had been totally destroyed.

The surface radiation was so intense they had to survey the ruined world from orbit. The continents were pitted and scarred. The ship's eight-inch telescope brought the surface so close they were practically walking through the empty streets of wrecked cities. To members of a race which had nearly met a similar fate, the sight was chilling.

"Some of this reminds me of the Horta," Jenorden said.

Roseka nodded. "I've been thinking the same thing."

"I think we taped some pictures of skeletons. Why don't we look them over and see if they look like the Horta? Maybe we can prove Macrella's theory."

"That ship the Horta had was pretty crude. Fifteen light years from where we found them is just about where I'd expect to find their home planet."

The evidence of the photographs wasn't conclusive, but Jenorden and Roseka agreed the skeletons would fit what they had seen of the Horta.

They moved on. As the months passed they discovered several inhabited worlds. Some they visited, and others they decided to leave alone.

Everything they learned was recorded in the ship's computer. Eventually all that knowledge, more than any single mind could hope to assimilate, would be added to the staggering load already in mankind's libraries.

Eight months after their encounter with the Horta, they entered a system near the center of the cluster. Veneleo gave an order and the ship began its contact program. Tracer beams swept the system in search of planets. Messages in every language in the computer, every language known to the human community and to every star-faring race the community had met, went out over hundreds of beams. All incoming radiation was analyzed by the computer for a pattern, and if it seemed to have one the pattern was compared, in seconds, with the entire language file. If any inhabitant of this system was broadcasting any language known to mankind, the computer would know before they came within ten million miles of a planet.

"Attention. Attention. We are receiving a message from the fourth planet."

The voice caught them all by surprise. They turned toward the wall speaker with renewed excitement.

"Star-farers!" Elinee said.

"Translation follows," the computer said. "Welcome from the Eb. Who are you? Please reply. End of message."

"What language?" Veneleo asked.

"Ungveerd."

"What part of the galaxy?"

"Sector Forty-nine."

Jenorden made a calculation. "About five thousand light years from here."

"Describe the race and the language," Veneleo said.

"Ungveerd. One language of a race of small, winged beings who live in the upper atmosphere of a giant, gaseous world. A sound language. Resembles whistling." The computer made some low whistling sounds to illustrate. "Note: this language is lacking in political concepts. Use as a common language with caution."

"Send the standard contact message," Veneleo said. "Prepare a learning program for Ungveerd."

They waited while the computer acknowledged the message it had received and whistled greetings and words of friendship from the visitors and from the human community. They all knew this could be the major discovery of their voyage. Since the computer had detected no message in Communal, the language of the human community, this had to be a star-faring race unknown to mankind.

"Message sent," the computer said. "Receiving message, Translation follows. Welcome from the Eb. Welcome from the three—next words precise translation impossible. Some land of political division. Continuing message. Welcome from their—next word precise translation impossible. Citizens? Inhabitants? Continuing message. Please excuse our linguistic crudities. Translation to Ungveerd difficult. Will you receive visual contact? End of message."

"Answer yes," Veneleo said.

Jenorden examined a group of instruments on the left side of the front wall. Detector beams were searching space for incoming missiles. Hatches had swung open and cannon had slid into firing position. The Horta were the only hostile star-farers mankind had ever encountered, and they were a special case, but in every meeting with technologically advanced races, reasonable precautions were taken.

The big screen in the center of the front wall flickered. The picture danced between sharp and blurry and then settled into focus. The four humans stood up.

Three beings appeared on the screen. They were roughly humanoid, with two arms, two legs, and a head which looked like it housed a brain and sense organs, but they were covered with thick fur. Their eyes were several times larger than human eyes, and they had small horns growing from their skulls. Two were covered with shiny brown fur, and one was white with black and white horns.

The brown Eb on the left touched his horns and said something in his own language. As he spoke, the computer provided a translation on a luminated strip under the screen.

"I am Nolten, Mentob of the Togme of Bel. Please call me Nolten."

That was the standard formula used by all star-faring people. A being gave his full name and title and then suggested a single name for the convenience of the aliens.

Question marks on the strip indicated the computer could not translate Mentob or Togme. The greetings of the other two Eb gave it a similar trouble. "I am Enrarkal," the second brown Eb said, "of the (nation? republic? democracy?) of Kroon. Please call me Enrarkal."

"I am Emcasa Mefala," the white one said, "of the (union? country? federation?) of Emcanes. Please call me Emcasa."

Veneleo bowed. "I am Veneleo Lenn, citizen of the human community. Please call me Veneleo."

One by one the other humans bowed and introduced themselves.

"Why do you come here?" Emcasa asked.

"To visit," Veneleo said. "To learn. To exchange knowledge with you, if you will. We are peaceful explorers. We will stay only if invited."

"Your ship is heavily armed."

"Only for defense. The weapons on this ship have never been used against any living creature. We will run before we will fight."

"We have powerful weapons," Nolten said. "If you attack us, we'll destroy you."

"He's making a threat!" Roseka said.

Jenorden glanced at the weapon board. From a star-faring race, threats, even defensive threats, were dangerously primitive behavior.

And the threats weren't the only evidence they had encountered something dangerous. If the computer had translated correctly, the Eb were still divided into political groups, something unheard of in a race which had advanced to interstellar travel. His stomach turned cold when he thought of a race equipped with the powerful technology faster than light travel required, and so savage it was still divided against itself.

"They aren't attacking," he said. "Keep up the diplomacy. I'll let you know if anything happens." He and Roseka both had their throat mikes off, so the computer wouldn't translate what they said.

"We will stay only if invited," Veneleo repeated. "You may take any precautions you wish."

"What did the others say?" Nolten asked. "Why wasn't that translated? I tell you we have weapons which can destroy planets. If we die, you'll die with us."

"Another threat," Elinee whispered.

"We are happy to meet such a powerful race," Veneleo said. "We wish to know you better. Tell us how we can satisfy your suspicions."

"You can't," Emcasa said. "Don't listen to him. All his people know is—"

"Silence!" Nolten said.

The screen blanked. Shocked by the same idea, the four humans stared at each other and then at the weapon board. "They can't be starfarers," Roseka said. "By now they would have blown themselves to bits."

"What do we do?" Veneleo asked. "Run or wait?"

For a moment no one spoke. They stared at the weapon board and thought the situation over, their powerful, disciplined brains examining every ramification before they made a decision.

"Wait," Jenorden said.

The other three nodded, one after the other.

The screen flickered. They watched it, Jenorden keeping one eye on the weapon board, and again it jiggled into focus.

The being who appeared on the screen was not an Eb. Neither was he humanoid. He had a lumpy body, with eyes, or something which looked like eyes, growing from it on top of long stalks; he had no hands, and, in fact, apparently had no grasping organs of any kind, and he stood on three legs. A striped skirt hung from his body to just above his knees. As soon as the screen came into focus, he bent his knees and spoke in a high, fast voice, the sound coming from a part of his body they couldn't see. Again a translation appeared on a luminated strip.

"I am Revliken Ziv, of the race of the Ivel, the Servants of the Borg. Please call me Revliken."

The humans were startled, but they went through the formula with their usual politeness and waited for the new being to continue.

"I am happy to meet you," Revliken said.

"Can you tell us what's happening?" Veneleo asked.

"This station on the fourth planet of this system belongs to the Borg. It was put here so the Borg could (announce? advertise? offer?) themselves to all visitors. However, since this is the system of the Eb, and since three Eb were present on this planet, I asked them to greet you. They have now asked me to greet you for them."

"Are the Eb a star-faring race?"

"The Eb are on the verge of travel within their own system. The group called the (nation? republic? democracy?) of Kroon—I think the translation will be crude, but I assure you it doesn't matter — that group recently orbited the Eb planet."

"Then your people are the star-farers?"

"The Ivel are the servants of the Borg."

"Who are the Borg?"

"The Borg inhabit a world in this cluster of stars. They invite all people to visit them. They will teach you anything you wish to know. Whatever your question, the Borg will answer it. My people travel the stars inviting every race to learn from the Borg. We build stations such as this one to inform all travelers of the existence of the Borg. I am about to take three representatives of the Eb to the world of the Borg. One of them, Emcasa Mefala, wants to learn how his race can avoid a world destroying war."

"The Borg will teach him that?"

"If the student wants to learn, the Borg will teach him anything."

Jenorden was shocked. He glanced at Roseka and Elinee and their faces told him they were just as shocked. Only Veneleo, because he was engaged in diplomacy, accepted the Ivel's words with a calm face.

Jenorden turned on his microphone. "Are you telling us you give advanced knowledge to primitives?"

"We are going to teach them how to make peace with themselves."

"Then you're going to teach them advanced social techniques!" The idea was so horrifying he had completely forgotten his manners. "That's worse than teaching them advanced technology."

"The Borg are teachers. All who wish to learn, may learn from the Borg."

"This disturbs us," Veneleo said. "Our race nearly died during a period of four hundred years in which new ideas and new technology were introduced faster than our society could adjust to them."

"Anyone may visit the Borg. I invite you to join the Eb and all the other people who are learning from the Borg."

"Why do the Borg do this?" Jenorden asked.

"The Borg will answer all questions."

"Can't you answer that one yourself?"

"The Borg have much to offer. Whatever troubles you, the Borg can help you. The Borg are the teachers. The Ivel are the servants of the Borg."

"But don't you know what advanced knowledge could do to a race like the Eb? How can you know how some piece of knowledge will affect a whole culture?"

"The Borg will answer all questions. Anything you wish to learn, come to the Borg, and the Borg will teach you."

"Where is this world?" Roseka asked.

"Tell me your system for giving directions in space."

"We'd better discuss this," Jenorden said. "Why don't we call him back?"

Veneleo glanced from face to face and took the consensus of the group. "Revliken, we want to discuss this. We'll call you back."

"I will wait for your call."

Veneleo turned off the transmission. They returned to their seats and spent several minutes thinking.

"I don't like it," Jenorden said. "The Eb can't even greet us without getting into a fight, and yet the Borg seem to think they can give them advanced knowledge without destroying them."

"I think we should visit the Borg," Roseka said. "If they can teach us something, we ought to learn it."

"But why would any race go to all this trouble?"

No one answered him. They were used to strange behavior and strange motivations, but this was something so alien they couldn't even speculate about it.

Chapter 4

They didn't like feeling suspicious. The emotion was so primitive it made them feel ashamed. But this was one encounter with an advanced race in which suspicion couldn't be dispelled. Any race which seemed to be tampering with the affairs of other cultures had to be approached with caution.

They had been discussing the situation for half an hour, when the computer announced they were receiving a broadcast from the fourth planet. Elinee switched on the screen and they saw the white Eb, Emcasa, standing by himself.

He started talking before they had time to bow. The words sped along the illuminated strip so fast they had trouble keeping up with them.

"I'm embarrassed by what happened. I know you must think we're savages but don't think all Eb are like Nolten. The Togme of Bel and the (republic? democracy? nation?) of Kroon are going to destroy the world if they aren't stopped. For the last twenty years they've been engaged in an arms race. They've developed terrible bombs and they're heading toward a war which will destroy us. The Borg are our only hope. The other two are going only because they're afraid the Borg will give us a new weapon. If they hadn't been allowed to come, the war would have started already. They threatened to destroy us if we didn't let them come."

They listened with blank faces and increasing horror. The situation on the Eb world was even worse than they had suspected. If it was really that bad, everything they said had to be preceded by careful thinking. Every word they spoke would be examined and pondered by the rival Eb factions. A few words from them which gave a wrong impression or accidentally revealed some minor bit of information could upset the delicate balance of power and trigger a catastrophe.

"We do not think you're savages," Roseka said.

"You're being kind, but I thank you. I hope I will see you on the Borg world. Now I have to—"

Somewhere behind Emcasa an Eb voice shouted. Nolten charged onto the screen and Emcasa whirled to meet him. They faced each other with their heads lowered and their horns pointed forward, a gesture which probably went back to the beginning of their race's history, and then Nolten put his hand in his fur and jerked out a two-pronged object which was undoubtedly a weapon.

"What's going on here?" Nolten demanded.

Emcasa stepped back. His head dropped even lower, pointing his horns at Nolten's stomach. The humans glanced at each other. Jenorden got a vivid picture of those sharp little horns stabbing upward into the belly of an enemy.

"I ought to kill you right here," Nolten said.

A door opened and shut and Revliken hopped into the camera's field of vision. "Stop him!" Emcasa said. "He's trying to kill me."

Revliken halted and faced the camera. His eye stalks moved slowly from Nolten to Emcasa.

"Take his weapon," Emcasa urged. "Hurry!"

"He was violating the treaty," Nolten said. "He was talking to the humans in secret. For all I know, he's already learned how to destroy us."

"You suspicious primitive! Why would they teach me anything? Can't you see how advanced they are? To them we're like children."

"We must return home at once," Nolten said. "You have broken the treaty. Revliken, you must return us to our planet." Emcasa turned on Revliken and gestured with both his hands. "He's been against this journey from the start. His people want me to fail."

"I insist we return," Nolten said.

Revliken bent his knees. "I will return you at once."

"You can't," Emcasa said. "You're our last hope. We're doomed. You can't let us die."

"Do you wish to return, Emcasa?" Revliken asked.

"Didn't you hear what I just said?"

"Do you wish to return, Emcasa?"

"No!"

Revliken bent his knees. "We will do what you wish."

"You just said you'd take us back," Nolten said.

"If you wish to go on, we will take you to the Borg. If you wish to return to your own world, we will return you."

"What about Emcasa?"

"We will do what he wishes."

"If he doesn't return with me, I'll kill him."

"He'll do it," Emcasa said. "Disarm him! Hurry!"

Revliken didn't answer. His lumpy body was as motionless as a rock.

"What are you waiting for?" Emcasa said. "What's wrong with you?"

"We cannot interfere," Revliken said.

Jenorden switched off his throat mike. "He can't interfere! What does he think he's doing?"

"Are you coming?" Nolten repeated.

"What's wrong with you?" Emcasa said. "You're destroying our last hope. You're dooming our entire race."

Again a door opened and shut off-screen. Enrarkal strode into the picture and his big Eb eyes passed slowly from the Ivel to the other two Eb and then to the humans.

"He was talking to the humans," Nolten said. "I caught him while he was doing it. He's violated the treaty."

"I see." Enrarkal gestured at the camera with his horns. "Have you asked the humans if they told him anything?"

"It doesn't matter. We're returning home."

"Emcasa has agreed?"

"If he doesn't go, I'll kill him."

"The Togme will be proud of you." Enrarkal touched horns at the humans. "Has Nolten asked you what happened?"

"Emcasa called us to apologize," Roseka said. "He told us about the situation on your world, and when he said we must think you're savages, I told him we don't. That's all any of us said to him."

"Do you still think we aren't savages?"

"Yes."

Enrarkal turned to Nolten. "Is there a record of the conversation?"

"He's violated the treaty," Nolten said. "We must return home."

"Revliken," Enrarkal asked, "is there a record of the conversation?"

"All broadcasts are automatically recorded."

Enrarkal turned to the humans. "I think we should discuss this without an audience." He touched horns and the picture faded and disappeared.

For a moment no one could speak. Their race, too, had once been divided into rival factions engaged in an arms race which could have ended in extermination. The Eb were at the beginning of a long time of troubles and no one could promise them they were going to survive.

"Revliken is just like a computer," Roseka said. "He only tells what he's asked. Emcasa could have died just because he didn't ask the right questions."

"After that scene," Jenorden said, "the Borg had better have proof they know what they're doing. The Eb can't even handle the knowledge they have, much less the kind of knowledge they're trying to get from the Borg."

They sat down in their swivel chairs. None of them looked comfortable. Their eyes kept glancing from the screen to the clock.

"This obligates us," Roseka said. "We have to investigate the Borg. I won't judge them in advance, and I don't see how any technologically advanced race could be that stupid, but judging by what we've just seen, the Borg could be a menace to every race in the galaxy."

An hour passed. One by one, they drifted out of the control room. They were worried but they were too alive not to grow bored waiting in front of a blank screen. Veneleo nibbled a buffet in the dining area; Roseka studied some of her observations on the last planet they had visited, and Elinee and Jenorden practiced an ancient duet they had uncovered in the ship's musical records. All the while a small part of each brain thought about the situation on the fourth planet and waited for news.

"Attention," the computer said. "Attention. We are receiving a message from the fourth planet."

In a moment they were all standing in the control room. Elinee switched on the screen and Revliken appeared before them and bent his knees.

"We are ready to leave," Revliken said. "Do you wish to visit the Borg?"

"Are the Eb going with you?" Jenorden asked.

"Yes."

"What are you going to teach them?"

"Nothing."

"What are the Borg going to teach them?"

"The Borg will teach them the answer to their question."

"Why didn't you tell Emcasa our conversation with him had been recorded?"

"We cannot interfere," Revliken said.

"Aren't you interfering by taking them to the Borg?"

"We don't consider that interference."

"Why not?"

"I cannot tell you."

"Why not?"

"You must ask the Borg."

"We've decided to visit the Borg," Veneleo said. "Our computer is about to broadcast our system for giving directions in space."

"Thank you. If you can give me some information on your language and your natural environment, we can have quarters prepared for you before you arrive."

"I'll have the computer broadcast that, too."

Revliken bent his knees. The screen blanked and they returned to the common. Roseka joined Veneleo at the buffet and Jenorden and Elinee continued practicing the duet. Again the shutters slid across the tall windows. Eating cakes and white meat, sipping delicate beverages and struggling with the complicated patterns of a shallow but interesting composer, they sped in minutes over distances light crossed in years.

They strolled to the control room as soon as the ship began to decelerate.

"Attention," the computer said. "Attention. We are receiving a message from the fourth planet."

"What language?" Veneleo asked.

"Communal."

"The Borg learn fast," Roseka said.

"Repeat the message," Veneleo ordered.

"Welcome from the Borg and from the Ivel, the servants of the Borg. Will you accept visual transmission?"

"Answer yes."

Jenorden switched on the screen. An Ivel appeared at once. "Welcome." The Ivel bent his knees. "I am Zilv Klenev, of the race of the Ivel, the servants of the Borg. Please call me Zilv."

Jenorden bowed. "I am Jenorden A'Ley, a citizen of the human community. Please call me Jenorden."

The others bowed and introduced themselves. "I am happy to meet you," Zilv said. "I will be your host and your guide as long as you are guests of the Borg. Quarters have already been prepared for you. We hope you will find them pleasant."

"We appreciate your courtesy," Veneleo said.

"Thank you. The Borg wish to give you as much of their knowledge as you desire. If you will tell me now what your questions are, we can begin preparing a learning program for you."

"The Borg answer all questions?" Roseka asked.

"Yes."

"How can I establish friendly relations with the Horta?"

"Who are the Horta?"

"A race we discovered several months ago. They're telepaths." She paused, but Zilv said nothing, and of course there was no way they could interpret his expression. "They use their powers to enslave other beings. When we tried to contact them, they nearly destroyed us."

"Can you give us a complete account of your encounter with the telepaths?"

"Certainly."

"I'll have our ship broadcast it right away," Veneleo said. "We will prepare a learning program for you. Are there any other questions?"

"Is this the first time you've heard anything about the Horta?" Jenorden asked.

"Yes."

"Then how can you teach us how to deal with them?"

"Whatever you wish to learn, the Borg will teach you."

Veneleo grinned. "How can I live forever and enjoy every minute of it?"

"We will prepare a learning program for you. Are there any other questions?"

"Tell me how I can save the Sordini," Elinee said.

"We will prepare a learning program for you. Do you have a question, Jenorden?"

He had expected to encounter many strange things when he had left Earth to explore the stars, but this—this calm, almost mechanical voice promising to teach the answer to all of life's problems—was so incomprehensible he wasn't sure it was real. "Only one," he said. "It isn't very profound, but since the Borg answer all questions, I'm certain they won't mind answering mine."

"Whatever you wish to learn, the Borg will teach you."

"Then tell me why the Borg are doing this."

"That is what you wish to learn?"

"This is what I wish to learn."

"We will prepare a learning program for you."

Chapter 5

Still cautious, they made a reconnaissance orbit of the Borg world. The planet was about half the diameter of Earth and about five light minutes from a small sun. The surface was an airless desert covered with large domes.

"The domes are quarters for our guests," Zilv Klenev informed them. "Yours is just south of the Borg dome. You'll see it in a moment. The Borg dome is the largest on the planet."

Jenorden checked the board. The domes were at least seventy miles in diameter and a mile high. The Borg dome, when it came over the horizon, was about three times the diameter of the other domes. The board said it was twelve miles high. To the naked eye it seemed to be filled with a yellow and green atmosphere.

The covenant of the human community made it immoral to leave the ship unattended. They could not risk having such power fall into the hands of beings who might not be qualified to control it. Leaving Elinee to be the first guard, they descended in two orbit-to-ground vehicles.

Zilv Klenev met them with a few courteous words and led them across the airless, dune-covered waste to the airlock. The surface of the dome was opaque and unrevealing. Taking no chances, Jenorden kept his left hand close to the button which activated his shield.

The outer door closed behind them. They waited, prepared for anything, and the inner door swung open. Jenorden started forward and then the hospitality of the Borg overwhelmed his senses and he halted with one foot inside the door. Beside him Roseka and Veneleo froze, too.

There was a broad, swift stream, and there was a lake, and there were woods and hills and fields. The gravity was Earth normal and the sky was Earth blue. In front of them, on the side of a hill, there was a rambling stone house.

Jenorden looked up. For the first time in eight years he saw white clouds sailing majestically across the sky.

"Do you like it?" Zilv asked. "If you want it modified, tell us."

"It's fine," Veneleo whispered.

"You can take your suits off if you wish. You don't have to fear disease."

Jenorden was so overcome his hand was on his zipper before he remembered the covenant. "We can't."

"Even if we've overlooked something and you get a disease, we can cure you."

"It would be immoral. We can't endanger the community. When you're dealing with disease there are too many unknown factors."

"How long did you have to prepare this?" Roseka asked.

"Six of your hours and nineteen of your minutes."

Jenorden was awed. No engineers known to mankind could equal the feat. The Borg might well be the most powerful race in the galaxy.

That night the scene looked more alien. The close, bright stars of the cluster filled the sky and the Borg dome dominated the horizon. Every time they looked out the rear windows of the house, they saw the giant yellow and green dome just over the top of the hill. Occasionally they glimpsed titanic black shapes, the Borg themselves.

Jenorden spent most of the hours after dinner staring at that lurid dome and brooding about what it meant. Even after he went to bed, he got up several times and went to the window.

They began their studies the next afternoon. Their classrooms, which Zilv had taken them through as soon as they were settled, were in a one-story building on the side of the hill. For each of them there was a room the size of an auditorium with a big spherical screen in the center and a variety of equipment grouped around a swivel arm chair.

A Borg appeared in the sphere as soon as Jenorden sat down. "Welcome, Jenorden A'Ley, citizen of the human community. Welcome. Welcome from all the Borg."

Peering through the thin yellow and green mist which surrounded the Borg, he could detect no exterior organs. The black shape seemed featureless. Judging by what he had seen the night before, the image was about a third actual size.

"Your hospitality is overwhelming," he said.

"Thank you. We hope you profit from your studies."

"Can you tell me how long they'll take?"

"That question will be answered during your program."

"Why can't you answer it now?"

"That question, too, will be answered during your program."

"I can't understand why you have to set up a complete program for a question every being who comes here must ask."

"You ask a great many questions, Jenorden."

"You present a great many mysteries."

"We want to teach you everything you wish to learn."

"Then when do you start giving me answers?"

"Now. May you profit from your studies."

The Borg disappeared. The lights went out and the screen darkened. In perfect Communal, a voice began describing the beginning of the universe. Light flickered through the black sphere. Clouds of radiant dust appeared and then the dust condensed into stars. Hosts of galaxies wheeled before his eyes.

The lecture was elementary, but it awed him even more than it had when he first studied the subject. As the spectacle unfolded, as the planets acquired life, and life acquired intelligence, and the first ships probed in each galaxy – and there were more galaxies in the universe than there were stars in any galaxy – the immensity of the drama evoked emotions so strong he sometimes forgot he was watching a screen. He was present at the actual creation of the cosmos.

A single galaxy filled the screen. The focus narrowed to a small yellow star and then to one planet. The calm, undramatic narrator listed the planet's major characteristics.

"Now we will study the history of the race which inhabits this world."

Again he was present at an awesome beginning, the birth of a world. Each stage in the planet's geological development was pictured and described. By the end of the second hour, the lecture had just arrived at the period in which intelligent life first appeared.

Jenorden pressed a button marked *Question*. An Ivel appeared and bent his knees.

"Why are you giving me this lecture?" Jenorden asked.

"That is a new question," the Ivel said. "We will have to prepare a new program."

"Why can't you just tell me?"

"That is a new question also."

"Would the new course be any shorter than this one?"

"I don't know."

"What are you people trying to do?"

"We are trying to serve the Borg."

"What are the Borg trying to do?"

"Jenorden, that is the question you originally asked."

He closed his eyes. "Continue the lecture."

Two hours later, having watched a race of blood sucking parasites begin to discover its newly mutated brain could be useful, he wandered into the next classroom and found Roseka was also watching the early history of an intelligent race. When she finally noticed him, she nodded and immediately returned her attention to the lecture.

In the next room Veneleo was watching a discussion between two beings so far from human in shape they made Jenorden feel visually disoriented. It was several minutes before he could see them clearly. They seemed to be arguing about the relationship between social organization and ocean-shaping. The discussion made little sense to him, but Veneleo was smiling and nodding his head. He tiptoed out of the room and went for a walk.

"Whatever the Borg are," Roseka said that evening, "they're master teachers. I don't think I could forget if I tried. And they did all this, setting up a program in our own language, in less than two days! I don't think any other race in the galaxy could do that."

"It's impressive," Jenorden said. "I'll be even more impressed when I start getting some answers. We've given them quite a list, haven't we? They're going to teach us how to deal with the Horta — even though they had to ask us who the Horta are — and Veneleo wants immortality, and they're going to tell Emcasa how to make peace..."

"It's hard to believe," Roseka said. "And yet, why go to all this trouble if they can't do it?"

"Why go to all this trouble if they *can* do it?"

"Maybe it's some form of amusement," Veneleo said. "It makes as much sense as exploring the galaxy, or writing music."

"Then why be so secretive about it?"

Chapter 6

Every day, he spent at least nine hours in the lecture room. If the Borg really intended to answer his question, he wanted to hear the answer soon.

He sat through the entire history of the blood sucking parasites, who died of disease only a few millennia after they acquired intelligence, and after that he again witnessed the birth of a world and the slow evolution of its life forms. This time the lecture on evolution went on several hours longer than the previous one had, and still no intelligent life form had appeared on the screen. Every minute detail, even the mating habits of obscure insects, was being included in the lecture. Exasperated, he pressed the question button and again demanded they tell him how long the program was supposed to last.

"How do I know this program has an end? How do I know you aren't trying to avoid answering me?"

"You don't," the Ivel said.

"Am I supposed to trust you?"

"If you wish to learn the answer to your question, you have to."

At the end of the ninth of the planet's twenty-seven hour days, he used the orbit-to-ground vehicle to travel to the Borg dome. Standing with his chin resting on his hand, he watched the giant black shapes appear and disappear among the shifting gases. He stayed there a long time, thinking and staring, and then he returned to his imitation Earth and sat in his sleeping room playing a group of harsh, passionate songs.

When he put down his bow, he left the house and walked down the hill to the dome Zilv lived in just inside the airlock. "I want to visit the other domes," he said. "Is that permitted?"

"Yes," Zilv said.

"Will you come with me and make the introductions?"

"I can come with you but I cannot interfere."

"What can you do?"

"I can answer questions."

"I'd like to start with the Eb. Can you tell me how I can contact them?"

"You can use the screen in your dome. You have to call the Ivel dome first and tell them what you want."

"If we go places where I don't know the language, can you act as interpreter?"

"Yes."

He used the next day, his turn to guard the ship, to learn all three Eb languages. It was hard work, even with drugs and the learning programs the computer prepared for him, but it was relief to get out of his suit. He did most of his learning while swimming naked in the pool.

He called the Eb the next morning. Emcasa and N. Rarkal—from his language studies he had learned Enrarkal was an incorrect rendering—both sounded pleased to hear from him. Nolten was courteous. When he suggested a visit, Emcasa told him he could come that afternoon. After a hurried conference the other two agreed.

The Eb dome was near the north pole and the trip took about two hours. Elinee and Zilv accompanied him.

The Eb greeting ceremonies were simple and brief. As they walked from the airlock to the Eb dwelling, making polite conversation, Jenorden learned something else about N. Rarkal. The emissary from the Republic of Kroon was a female, or at least of the child bearing sex.

The Eb dwelling was a circular metal wall. Inside the wall, each inhabitant seemed to have a small covered dwelling of his own. Their hosts led them to a shallow pit in the center of the ring and as soon as they were all seated around the edges of the pit, Jenorden and Emcasa began exchanging information.

Emcasa had been spending ten to twelve hours a day in the lecture room, with Nolten and N. Rarkal keeping watch on him, and he was obviously growing impatient. His complaints were vehement. He, too, had asked the Borg how long his program was going to take, and received no answer. Since his arrival, he had been watching a lecture on the evolution of a race with a history very similar to the history of the Eb. Then, just this morning, as the lecture reached the moment when the race developed weapons of mass destruction, the subject had changed. He was now watching the evolution of a race so unlike the Eb it had seventeen sexes and the entire planet was one consciousness.

"Did you ever think of asking them my question?" Jenorden asked.

"Many times," N. Rarkal said.

"You can't understand how I feel," Emcasa said. "When they came to us it was a gift from the sky. All I could think of was saving my people."

"Do you still think the Borg can help you?"

"I have to."

"What do you think, N. Rarkal?"

"I don't think anything," N. Rarkal said. "How can I? We're dealing with the unknown. The Borg may give us information we can use and then again they may not. Even if they tell us something, it will probably do more harm than good."

He turned to Nolten. "What do you think?"

"Evaluation isn't my job," Nolten said.

"That's the attitude," Emcasa said. "His people all think like that. That's why their precious Togme is leading them straight into suicide. I can imagine how stupid we must seem to beings like you."

Embarrassed, Jenorden returned to discussing what the Borg had been teaching Emcasa. The world consciousness on the planet Emcasa was currently studying sounded fascinating. He tried to get more details, but after a few minutes the conversation suddenly turned into a tirade by Emcasa on the follies of the Eb.

N. Rarkal interrupted with an impatient-looking gesture with her horns. "Perhaps our guests would like some entertainment."

"Thank you," Jenorden said. "That's very thoughtful of you. It sounds to me like we've discussed everything we can."

"Do you enjoy the hunt?"

Emcasa made a strange sound. "The humans are civilized people! I'm sorry, Jenorden. I'm sorry she offended you. On her part of our world, they still kill animals for amusement."

N. Rarkal jumped to her feet. "You insulting boor!"

Her head lowered and her horns pointed straight at Emcasa's chest. Jenorden and Elinee glanced at each other. Jenorden's calves and thighs tensed slightly and he primed himself to jump backward out of the pit.

"The treaty," Nolten shouted. "N. Rarkal!"

N. Rarkal didn't move. Emcasa stood up and the two of them faced each other across the diameter of the pit.

"Emcasa Mefala," N. Rarkal said, "if it weren't for the treaty I'd kill you here and now."

Emcasa turned to Jenorden. "That's our basic problem. The two most primitive countries have the strongest weapons. No other country wanted to make such things."

"What do you hunt?" Jenorden asked N. Rarkal.

N. Rarkal raised her head. "An animal called the herkan. We breed it so it will be as dangerous as possible."

"What's it like?"

"Would you like to look at one?"

"Certainly."

"I'll have to drive us there. They're a few miles down the road."

"If we hunt them, can I use my own weapon?"

"Of course. You can decide for yourself if it's good enough."

He bowed. "Thank you."

"Do you hunt on your world?"

"We do whatever we please."

"You sound like you've been lucky."

"We have been. I'm sorry I can't tell you more."

"I'll get a car. I'll meet you outside in a minute."

"Are you really going to hunt this animal?" Elinee asked in Communal.

"I may. I'll decide after I've looked at it."

"You can't resist a new experience, can you?"

"I won't do it if it looks too dangerous."

She smiled. "I can't believe you."

He turned to Emcasa and Nolten. "Are you coming with us, honored gentlemen?"

"I have to," Nolten said.

"Of course," Emcasa said. "Certainly."

N. Rarkal drove them to the herkan in a noisy open car. The dome was as spacious as the dome the Borg had provided the humans but it was much colder and the vegetation was a darker green. Jenorden had to raise the temperature of his suit twice before they reached a long, flat building several minutes' drive from the Eb dwelling.

He wondered if he was really going to hunt with N. Rarkal. It wasn't as obvious as Elinee thought. Already he could feel an odd numbness in his arms and legs and a strange sensation in the pit of his stomach, the fear he had learned about but had never felt very strongly until the day he fought the Horta.

When they entered the building they were greeted by wild shrieks, the noise of huge bodies thrashing against metal bars, and the whir of many wings. The clamor evoked primitive, disturbing emotions in Jenorden's psyche, but he and Elinee looked around them with their usual air of calm. They were standing at one end of a bare, well lighted corridor. On each side of the corridor were big cages with thick, iron bars, and in each cage, shrieking at them and angrily beating several pairs of stubby wings, was a long, many legged animal.

The animal closest to the door had pulled itself up the front of its cage and was holding itself erect by gripping the bars with its foremost pairs of legs. Looking down on them it shrieked and tried to push its blunt, primitive face between the bars.

The teeth were bad enough. They looked as vicious as any teeth Jenorden had seen on any living creature in the galaxy. But even worse than the teeth were the two sets of claws, mounted on short arms, which grew from the fur on each side of the face. As they watched, the animal turned its head and got one set of claws between the bars. The long nails moved up and down and it was unpleasantly easy to imagine them raking living flesh.

"They certainly look deadly," Jenorden said.

N. Rarkal led them down the corridor. "They are deadly. They're the best opponents a brave man can have." She paused in front of a cage. "You can't see them until they leap. When they charge, they're faster than a car, and when they leap, the wings add to their speed. We added the wings and the face claws by breeding."

"That's quite a feat."

"Thank you. We also increased their intelligence. By the best measure we've got, they're twice as intelligent as any other animal on our planet. When they hunt together, they cooperate. Only suicides ever hunt more than two or three at once."

Jenorden's hand kept straying to his pistol. Elinee was right. He couldn't resist a new experience.

"The hunting ground is right outside," N. Rarkal said. "Inside that stone wall. The Borg built us a big one. To hunt them all you do is walk through it. Sooner or later you see a ripple in the grass. That's the herkan hunting you. You get one shot when it leaps."

"Are you going to hunt with her?" Elinee asked Jenorden in Communal.

"She hasn't repeated her invitation." He smiled. "That's the most considerate thing she's done so far."

"It's unbelievable," Emcasa said. "Visit their country and this is all you hear: who's the best hunter, who breeds the most vicious animals, when the next public hunt will be. It's hard to understand, isn't it? I suppose it's been thousands of years since your people behaved like that."

Jenorden stared at the row of cages. He wondered how Emcasa would react if he told him it had only been four hundred years since the period when sober observers had been afraid the human race was going to destroy itself in a thermonuclear war.

He stared at the row of cages. One shot... His reflexes were good and so was his coordination. He was probably a better, faster shot than any Eb now living. He had the advantage of all the improvements two centuries of genetic engineering had made in the human physique, plus a life span so long he had been able to spend leisurely decades training his body.

The herkan shrieked and pushed against the bars. Its eyes glared at him with angry cunning.

"Are you ready for the hunt?" he asked N. Rarkal.

"You'll join me?"

"Yes."

She stared at him. "I wonder what you're feeling right now. Forgive my bad manners, but that expressionless accent of yours conceals the biggest mystery I've ever encountered. What kind of being has all the powers you have and can still enjoy the hunt?"

"I'm sorry I'm a mystery to you. I'd like to be your friend."

"In my country when two people hunt the herkan together, they're friends for life, no matter what else comes between them."

He bowed. "Thank you. I'm honored."

"We'd better go now. It's getting late."

She started walking toward the door. As they passed each cage, the animal inside shrieked and threw itself against the bars.

"I let a herkan loose in the field two days ago," N. Rarkal said. "By now it should be ready for us, hungry but not weak."

She led him to the high wall behind the building. Together they lifted a ladder and placed it against the chilly stone. She drew a double barreled pistol from under her fur and examined it, and Jenorden drew his own weapon and had Elinee make sure his converter was all right.

They went up the ladder. For a moment he stood on the wall and looked around, taking in the open sky and the long sweep of grassy field in front of him. The sun was to their left and behind them and the clouds were slowly changing color, from light orange to deep red.

"I always stop, too," N. Rarkal said.

"Can Elinee stand here while we're hunting?"

"Certainly. She'll be safe."

He waved to Elinee and she came up the ladder with Nolten behind her. Zilv and Emcasa looked like they were going to stay on the ground and then Emcasa made a gesture Jenorden couldn't interpret and he came up the ladder, too.

N. Rarkal shaded her eyes with her hand. "Look for ripples in the grass. If you don't see any, our adversary is at the other end. They never stop moving."

They pulled up the ladder and let it down the inner face of the wall. N. Rarkal went down first, while Jenorden watched the field for her. Gun ready, she crouched at the foot of the ladder. Jenorden turned to Elinee and let his face reveal all his complex feelings, including his awareness he might never be this close to Elinee or any other woman, again.

"Jenorden..." She tried to show him what she felt and then she shook her head hopelessly. "I'd have to make a speech to tell you how I feel."

"I know." He squeezed her hand. "Tonight. We'll go back to the ship."

"Yes." She looked at him with a tenderness he had seen only a few times before, and then only when they were alone together.

He climbed down the ladder and he and N. Rarkal moved forward. Waist-high grass rustled against the fabric of his suit.

"Don't relax your guard for a moment," N. Rarkal said. "This isn't a game. The herkan was bred to be a fit adversary for warriors." Her eyes traversed the field as she talked. "Did I tell you to aim for the head? That's the only place you can kill them."

He and Roseka had a big job waiting for them. He did not know a single normal, healthy human who risked his life simply for the excitement of it. Anything so unusual had to be analyzed until every suspicion of sickness had been allayed.

He froze. With his left hand he pointed at a far off movement in the grass.

N. Rarkal lowered her head. "Let's spread apart." She edged away from him and he moved the other way until they were several yards apart. They crouched above the grass and watched the oncoming ripple. The grass moved so violently it was easy to imagine the huge body running along the ground. As N. Rarkal had told him, it moved quite a bit faster than her car.

"He's attacking you, Jenorden."

He nodded. His legs wanted to tremble, but his brain had them under control. The ripple stopped. Confused, he tried to look where it had been.

"This one's a coward," N. Rarkal called. "Stay alert. He may not charge until he's almost on us."

"What if he's circling us?"

"Move this way. We'd better stand back to back."

He edged toward her, making a complete turn every step. His back felt naked. No matter which way he looked, he felt certain the animal was coming at him from another direction.

For several minutes they stood back to back in the middle of the field. Somewhere, moving so slowly and gently not a blade of grass was disturbed, the herkan was creeping along on its belly. The wall, with Elinee and the others silhouetted on top of it, looked like something in a far off dream.

"Do they do this often?" he asked.

"We've drawn a bad one. Now and then we get one like this."

"Is he trying to wear us down?"

"He could be. They can be very intelligent."

"How many have you killed?"

"Fourteen. I've been on more hunts, but on the others the people I was with did the killing."

"How often does the herkan kill the hunter?"

"Often enough to make it dangerous."

Two hundred yards away, perhaps three hundred, the grass moved. It could have been the wind or a trick of his eyes. He tried to focus on the place where he had seen it.

The herkan leaped from the grass. Shrieking with all the power of its lungs, it hurtled toward him with its wings beating and its claws fully extended.

He brought his gun up. N. Rarkal had been right. He would have one shot. And he couldn't fire hastily, either. He had to aim. In less than three seconds he had to get the head and eyes between the sights, and he had to calculate the proper lead and step out of the way the moment he fired. Even the dead animal could kill him.

The head disappeared. He fell to one side and the body hurled past him and crashed into the ground.

N. Rarkal was yelling at him. "Good! Good! Wonderful! You didn't have any warning at all! Magnificent!"

He was lying flat on the grass. His fingers felt so numb he couldn't grip the butt of his pistol. He raised his head and looked thankfully at the sky.

He stood up and shoved his gun into its holster. A furred hand touched his wrist. Two big eyes studied his face.

He squeezed her hand. He was too full of emotion to worry about what the gesture might mean to her.

He walked to the body and stared at it. This wasn't the first time he had killed an animal. During his education he had been required to slaughter several meat animals with his own hands, and he had also had to watch the painless slaughter machines do the job. It was unhealthy to eat meat and repress the knowledge it was the flesh of killed animals.

It would have been equally unhealthy to have killed and not contemplated the consequences of his act. Squatting in the grass flattened by the huge carcass, he examined the mangled head, and ran his eyes along the length of the body. There had been something terrible and magnificent in the universe and now it was gone.

"What are you doing?" N. Rarkal said.

"It's a ritual my people have."

"You contemplate your victory? You think about your courage?"

"Something like that."

"I'm sorry. I think I'm prying."

"I'm sorry I can't be more open. What do you do with the herkan after you kill it?"

"We clear the ground and burn the body where it lies."

"I'll help you."

They labored together, uprooting the grass for several yards around the body so the fire wouldn't spread. They burned the animal until its bones were bare of flesh and then they kicked dirt and cold ashes on the skeleton and returned to the wall.

As he stepped onto the wall Elinee gave him her hand. Her face expressed emotions even more complex and varied than they had been when he left her.

"Roseka and I have a lot to talk about," Jenorden said.

"Do you feel guilty?"

"I don't think so. I'll have to talk to Roseka."

N. Rarkal drove them to the airlock. As they were saying goodbye, Emcasa suddenly asked Jenorden if he could accompany the humans when they visited the other domes.

"My government sent a pressurized tractor with me but it's too slow. Will there be room in your craft?"

"Won't Nolten and N. Rarkal object?"

"We certainly will," Nolten said. "If he leaves the dome, we have to go with him."

"I can't take all of you, Emcasa. Our vehicle only holds six, and there'll be two or three of us and you'll be wearing bulky suits."

"Will you do it if the others let me go alone?"

Jenorden thought. He was certain Nolten and N. Rarkal would veto the idea.

"All right. If the others don't object, we'll take you with us."

"We'll talk it over," Emcasa said. "I'll call you when we decide."

Chapter 7

"I think we've discovered why you're doing this," Roseka said. "Now we have to determine if it's healthy."

Jenorden slumped onto his spine. The struggle to understand his emotions had always been hard for him and these last two hours had been even harder than usual.

"What do you think?" Roseka asked. "Do you think it's healthy?" She was pacing the floor, as she often did when she questioned them.

"I wouldn't if I were doing it out of cruelty or because I want to die. But I'm not. And the animal isn't a substitute for something I hate and can't admit I hate, either."

"We've eliminated all those motivations, all right. But still, do you think it's unhealthy?"

He shook his head slowly.

"Are you sure?" Roseka asked.

"No, and neither are you."

"Do you want to go hunting again?"

"Not now. In a few days I may want to."

"You've got a complex group of emotions this thing satisfies. Excitement. Pleasure in your own competence. That other feeling, that intensifying of sensory impressions. And of course there's the conflict that's probably the basis of most of your personality — your hunger for life versus your feeling that life is futile. You want to face death partly because you're afraid your idea that life is pointless will someday make you an unfeeling robot. You want to confront that fear and struggle with it. Are there any emotions there you're ashamed of?"

"I'm not exactly proud of what you call my sense of futility. But that isn't a motivation. I'm going hunting so I can fight that. I have a feeling I *should* be ashamed, and yet every time I face danger I feel as if I'm learning something. This is an experience very few humans have anymore. Who knows what the standards are?"

"Are you willing to be analyzed every time you do it?"

He thought for a moment. "I'm not sure I think it's worth it."

"I don't think you should hunt if you aren't willing to be analyzed every time you come back from it."

She was right. He hated analysis but he knew this was something they had to observe carefully. Any behavior this unusual was as potentially dangerous to the community as a new virus.

"It looks like I have to," he said.

He was glad the next day was Roseka's turn to guard the ship. After two restless hours in the lecture room, he went for a long hike. He stayed out all day. When it rained in the late afternoon, he stood in a meadow and tried to pretend the water was running down his skin instead of his suit.

When he returned from the hike Elinee told him Emcasa had called. Nolten and N. Rarkal had agreed he could accompany the humans on their travels.

"I wonder how he did that," Jenorden said.

"I couldn't tell. When are you going to start?"

"I was thinking about tomorrow. Do you mind if I start without you? Tomorrow's your day on the ship, isn't it?"

"You'll have to do some of your exploring without me anyway."

N. Rarkal called shortly after sundown. "We hunted together," she said, "and therefore I trust you in spite of the gulf between us. If Emcasa does anything or learns anything which may be dangerous, will you tell us at once?"

"Certainly," Jenorden said. "I'll call you after every trip and tell you everything that happened."

"He made such a fuss about it I finally said he could do it if you agreed to watch him for us. He said he'd go exploring in his tractor without us, and of course if he did that Nolten would insist we return to our own world."

"Don't you want to return to your own world?"

"Not yet. I come from an adventurous people. I don't know if the Borg will teach us how to make peace, but if I had to leave now, I'd be very disappointed."

"Suppose Emcasa learns something that will be dangerous even if you know he knows it?"

"We can always kill him. He knows the risk he's taking."

Her matter of fact tone chilled him. After he switched off the screen, he spent a long time staring out the window at the Borg dome.

He and Zilv left early in the morning. When they arrived at the Eb dome, they landed just outside the airlock and a moment later Emcasa appeared in a spacesuit which was just as clumsy as Jenorden had expected. They had to wait patiently while their encumbered guest plodded across the waste and struggled up the ladder. When he entered the cabin his features were completely hidden behind a tiny, dark face plate.

"Where are we going first?" Emcasa radioed.

"Just a few domes away," Jenorden said. "The less time we spend traveling, the more time we can spend learning something."

"Do you think we'll learn anything important?"

Jenorden glanced south. He couldn't see the Borg dome from here, but he could picture every detail of it and the image sent a rush of emotion up his spine. The Borg could not have challenged him more if they had stood before him with sighted weapons and threatened to kill him.

"Sooner or later," he said. "We may not like what we learn, but even the Borg can't hide something from us forever."

That day they visited a race so primitive the four or five living in the dome seemed to think the Borg were gods and that they had been transported to the afterlife they believed in. "How can we become gods, too?" they had asked.

Shy as animals, they spoke to Jenorden by shouting from deep inside a cave. Their language, which Zilv translated into Emcanes and Communal, seemed to have a rudimentary vocabulary. Many of Jenorden's questions couldn't be translated — or at least Zilv said they couldn't be.

Soon Jenorden had completely given up the Borg learning program. He was certain it would be years, if ever, before he learned anything in that lecture room. They were still showing him lectures on minute details of the history of every culture of the second race they wanted him to study. He might not learn anything exploring the domes, but even if he didn't, his explorations might eventually force the Borg to try and stop him, and thus reveal something of their motives.

During the next few weeks they visited several domes. Jenorden soon observed an obvious pattern. Most of the beings living in the domes had asked for power, or for some knowledge which would give them power, and the Borg had begun their education by teaching them history and philosophy.

There was, for example, a group of beings who called themselves the Ersar-Aswero *crar*. They represented the dormant political division of their race and they had asked the Borg how their government could conquer the rest of their world. For three years they had been studying philosophy and history. They were getting impatient, but their rulers had told them to go to the Borg planet and do what the Borg told them until they were ordered to return, and their rulers were never disobeyed. A primitive race, armed with cross bows and swords and wearing armor, their social system apparently used the most primitive techniques for getting people to cooperate.

For a while Jenorden was fascinated by them. They seemed to have some kind of herd instinct, which was rare in intelligent races. They reproduced in groups of sixteen males or sixteen females, and each group remained together all its life, uniting with a group of the opposite sex to produce a mature *crar*. When they talked to their visitors, they talked as a group and reacted as a group. Swiftly, without any regard for manners, one would speak, and then another would comment, or even interrupt, and the process of thinking would flow through the group as if it were traveling along one nervous system, until finally a consensus was stated. Their greeting ceremonies were precise, complicated drills which were executed without anyone giving orders.

Roughly humanoid, they were thick skinned and about five feet tall. Because their brain was located in their torso, where it was protected by their thick, armored chests, their head was just a tiny lump on top of their body, a lump with a mouth, a breathing organ in the rear, ears on the side, and two tiny eyes covered with a hard, transparent substance. Their muscles looked powerful. They moved in long bounds, covering so much ground with each stride that they were several times faster than a running human.

Their world was dark and rugged, with winds so strong there was a constant flow of grit and small rocks occasionally flew through the air. They had just started using windmills to generate electricity.

In the dome next to the Ersar-Aswero lived a lone being who belonged to a race which appeared to be at least as advanced as the human community. "Please call me Rotrudo," he greeted them. "I have a few other names, but that's good enough." He was almost three times the height of a human. His arms and legs were long and skinny and his head seemed ridiculously small on such a large body.

According to his own words, he had been on the planet more than fifty years. He was so gentle and courteous Jenorden was amazed to learn he had asked the Borg how he could become the ruler of the galaxy.

"Repeat my question, Zilv! Are you sure you translated correctly?"

"My translation is correct. Your language and his are very similar. Your word ruler and the word I translated ruler have almost the same semantic content."

"Ask him if he really expects the Borg to teach him that."

"What kind of madness is this?" Emcasa asked.

"I used to doubt the Borg," Rotrudo answered, "but I don't any more. Thirty local years ago I asked them how long it was going to take and they told me another hundred and sixty local years. I consider an answer that discouraging evidence of their sincerity. If they had been trying to encourage me to stay here, they would have told me it would take much less."

"Don't you think they may have known you would think that way?"

"Perhaps. But how can the members of one race understand a single member of another race that well? I can't believe it."

"Do you think you've learned anything about their motives?"

"For many years now they have been teaching me the customs, history and philosophy of many races. I am certain they are giving me a moral preparation before they give me the power to establish my rule. If I succeed, I will be a wise ruler."

They talked for a long time. Long before they finished, Jenorden decided Rotrudo's question wasn't as insane as it had first appeared. Rotrudo had contemplated the chaos of the galaxy during many years of wandering, and he had decided one consciousness must eventually establish its rule and bring order to the pointless flowering of intelligent life.

"The galaxy must have a purpose," he said, "and only a single consciousness can give it a purpose. And no group of races could ever determine a single purpose. Only one consciousness completely devoted to this single aspect of life, can hope to be successful. The need is great! All over the galaxy intelligent beings are dying of despair. Entire races lose their passion to live and create as soon as they leave their native worlds and learn how immense their environment is."

"Agreed," Jenorden said. "But if the Borg can teach you what you've asked, why don't they rule the galaxy themselves?"

"I've wondered about that many times. Before I leave here I'll probably know."

"How much of your life span are you gambling?"

"I will have less than a century to live when I leave here." Emcasa made a growling sound which meant he was startled. Both human faces showed horror at such a commitment of life.

"What have you asked the Borg?" Rotrudo asked.

"I asked them why they're doing all this."

"And they gave you a learning program, and you grew impatient and decided to visit the rest of us and see if you could find out by yourself."

"Yes."

"Have you some other goal which makes you impatient to move on?"

"Yes. I want to visit every star, learn everything there is to learn, and experience everything there is to experience."

"And you thought I was insane."

Jenorden laughed. "At least I'm not cooped up in a dome."

"Sometimes this dome seems bigger than the galaxy. Give the Borg a chance. Go back to your dome and study for a few years. See if you don't come to have faith in them."

"The Borg bring some extremely primitive races here," Elinee said. "Doesn't that bother you? Even if they give their students years of moral preparation, how can they be certain a particular individual has grown enough to handle the knowledge they can give him? How can they understand so many strange psychologies that well?"

"I believe the Borg know what they're doing."

"Why?"

"Have you ever seen or heard of a race as powerful as the Borg?"

"That doesn't mean they can do everything," Jenorden said.

"Doesn't it make you think they can do anything they claim they can do?"

"But what are they getting from all this?"

"Why do you explore the stars?"

"To learn. To experience. We get something every place we go. What are they getting?"

Emcasa put a heavy, gauntleted hand on Jenorden's shoulder. "Jenorden, excuse me. It's late."

Jenorden nodded. "We have to go, Rotrudo."

"Visit me again. I have something I'd like to show you. My race has a work of art—our only one, it replaced all the others we've created—which we think is the ultimate expression of our being. Would you like to see it?"

"Yes," Elinee said. "Very much. It sounds exciting."

Rotrudo showed them to the airlock. Emcasa looked worried, but Elinee took the controls as soon as they were settled in the vehicle, and they made a perfect airless landing beside the Eb dome less than an hour after they left Rotrudo.

Emcasa struggled to his feet. "Jenorden, will you walk to the dome with me? I'm afraid I may run out of air."

"Certainly."

He followed Emcasa into the airlock and they walked across the harsh wasteland to the dome. His muscles ached with the effort it took to move as slowly as the bulky spacesuit made Emcasa walk.

"I want to ask you something," Emcasa radioed. "I have a favor to ask. We can talk in private here. You know what the situation is on my world. You know a race is about to die. A whole race! A thousand million intelligent beings! Does our fate arouse your pity?"

"More than you'll ever know. What do you want? You don't have to make speeches, Emcasa."

"I know the Borg can't help us in time. Our race may be extinct already. Believe me, we were on the verge of extinction when we left home."

"Go on." Jenorden tried to keep his voice flat and noncommittal.

"You have to help us. Only you can help us."

"You don't understand. Anything we give you will do more harm than what you already have."

"I do understand. I don't want you to give us weapons. I have as little faith in my people as you do."

"Then what do you want?"

"Come and rule us. *Make* us stop fighting. *Make* us unify. I saw how powerful the Borg ship is and I know your ship is just as powerful. You can do it. No weapon we have can stop you. You could orbit our planet and train your weapons on us. If any country did anything which would lead to war, you could destroy them. And once we'd disarmed and were living in peace — it would only take a few years — then you could leave us."

Jenorden felt sick. Killing in self-defense was tolerable, but mass slaughter, even thinking about threatening mass slaughter, was revolting. In the first years of his education he had been taught a moral principle which he couldn't forget. He could kill one or two or even ten in self-defense, but at some point there was a limit to the price he could set on his own life. The Eb hadn't learned that yet, and therefore they were in danger, but it was up to them to prove their competence. If they failed, they weren't fit to continue evolving. There was no room in the universe for people who could build powerful weapons and then couldn't control themselves enough to survive their own ingenuity.

"We can't." He put a hand on the spacesuited shoulder. "I'm sorry. Don't ask me to explain why. We can't."

"Don't you care what happens to us?"

"Goodbye, Emcasa."

He turned on his heel. A gauntleted hand reached for his shoulder but he evaded it and strode toward the ship. "Jenorden! I beg you!"

There was nothing he could do. He couldn't even tell them the terrible truth that in this test they were alone and success was not guaranteed. Learning that was part of the test. "Monster! Insect! You have the passions of an insect!"

He trudged up the ladder. He radioed Elinee to take off while he was still inside the airlock.

That evening he called the Eb dome and told Emcasa he couldn't accompany them anymore. That should have been clear already, but Emcasa made a long oration, growing more and more emotional, until he had to cut him off to preserve his sanity. A little later N. Rarkal called and said she hoped they were still friends.

"We are," Jenorden said. "I'm surprised you asked. We hunted the herkan together. Your people are right—that makes you friends for life."

"Things aren't as bad on our world as Emcasa likes to think. We'll solve our problem, and we don't need help to do it, either. My race isn't going to die."

"I hope he doesn't do something that forces you to return to your own world. I kept on taking him with me primarily because you want to stay here. I don't think it did any harm, but I never was comfortable about it."

"He'll calm down. When are we going hunting again?"

"I think I'd better wait awhile. Invite me as soon as you think it's all right."

"I will. Good hunting, Jenorden."

"Good hunting, my friend."

Chapter 8

The stone was as passionate and mysterious as a human face. Revolving on a thick disk, in the center of a blue room where Rotrudo, Elinee and Jenorden sat in three niches in the wall, it turned with all the slow, impressive massiveness of a world suspended in space. Each of its hundreds of facets was a different color and texture, and through some trick of the effects of moving colors no facet looked the same for more than an instant. The rough became shiny, and the shiny warm, and dark places which drew them in suddenly exploded. It was only color and texture blended by rotary motion — the technology was so elementary even the electric motors of the Ersar-Aswero could have handled it — but it pulled tides of emotion through Jenorden's psyche. All the while he watched it he seemed to hear music.

Beside him Elinee gasped. He knew what she was thinking. Was this the kind of work her imagination was creating? Was something like this, the ultimate expression of her race, to come from her mind?

The last revolution ended. There was a long silence and then Rotrudo pushed himself out of his niche. "Thank you. I hope you enjoyed it."

Elinee glanced at Jenorden. "We did," she said. "We both enjoyed it very much. Thank you."

"Do you experience this often?" Jenorden asked.

"Every few days. That's more than I'd need if I weren't living alone."

"You're a strange person, Rotrudo."

"No stranger than life itself. Have you been attending your lectures?"

"Not since the last time we saw you."

"And that was twenty local days ago, at least. By now the Borg might have answered your question."

"I'd like to agree with you, but I doubt it."

Rotrudo gave an order. The wall opened and they stepped outdoors. A brown fog had settled around the house while they were inside.

"I wish I could invite you again," Rotrudo said. "I've enjoyed having company."

"We may never see you again?"

"You're the last people I intend to see from now on until I finish my studies."

Overcome with emotion, Jenorden hunted for words. Finally he reached up and gripped Rotrudo's wrist. The alien flesh felt hot, and to the other his suit probably felt cold and hard, but Rotrudo stooped a little and put a hand on his shoulder, and something of what they felt passed between them.

"Do you mind if I don't walk you to the airlock?" Rotrudo asked.

"We can make it ourselves. You go back to work."

They turned away. Thoughtfully they plodded through the mist. Just inside the airlock Zilv met them outside a small Ivel dome. They entered the airlock and waited patiently while it cycled, and then they hiked across the dunes to their vehicle.

Elinee was the first to enter the cabin. Jenorden followed behind her, thinking about Rotrudo and paying little attention to his surroundings. Suddenly Elinee gasped. He jerked out of his reverie and his eyes darted from her face to where she was looking.

The control panel was a wreck. The instruments had all been shattered and the wheel was lying on the seat with its shaft and control wires cut through.

He stepped forward, and bent over the wreckage. The radio had been attacked, too. The vehicle couldn't operate and they couldn't possibly radio for Veneleo to bring them the second vehicle.

Elinee put a hand on his back. "What does it mean?"

He straightened up and glanced around the cabin. Zilv was squatting placidly on the rear seat. Through the window he could see nothing but lifeless dunes, black sky, and Rotrudo's dome.

"Can we use Zilv's radio?" Elinee asked. "Zilv, can you contact one of your people?"

"No," Zilv said. "My radio has too short a range."

Jenorden shrugged. They had both seen the Ivel dome just inside Rotrudo's dome, but of course there might not be an Ivel in it.

"Let's go back to the dome," he said. "We'll use Rotrudo's equipment."

He turned to go, and then a movement among the dunes caught his eye. A strange vehicle was approaching the two dunes which rose between the vehicle and Rotrudo's airlock. As soon as he saw it, he put the facts together and understood what was happening.

The vehicle was a rough wooden deck suspended between four wheels. Half a dozen Ersar-Aswero, in full armor and carrying crossbows, were holding onto a wooden railing. At the rear of the deck was an electric motor and a tall cylinder which had to be a device, probably a wet cell, for generating electricity.

Taking out binoculars, he studied the vehicle and its passengers. The Ersar-Aswero had managed to convert their armor into crude space suits. A pair of oversized air tanks burdened each back. Somehow they had managed to design airtight joints which were flexible but which wouldn't let the internal pressure spread-eagle the suit.

The vehicle halted and the Ersar-Aswero jumped off and bounded stiffly to positions behind the dunes. They couldn't have run in those suits—it took them most of the time they were in the air to bend their knees for the landing—but with their long bounds they could cover the ground almost as fast as when they were unencumbered in their own environment.

They couldn't reach the dome without a fight. They could turn on their shields and run the gauntlet, but if Rotrudo didn't open up the airlock soon after they reached it, they might be trapped in the open with no energy left in their converters.

He lowered the binoculars and looked around. Directly in front of the vehicle's nose, a second group was dismounting from another flat car and taking up positions. Still another group had been rolling up behind him while he was watching the group in front of the dome. They were surrounded, or would be in a moment.

"They can't be planning to attack us," Elinee said.

"Not with crossbows. And they can't be planning to outwit us either, not with those suits." He scanned the area. "They must have something else. Shall we wait here or shall we run for the dome? Can you open Rotrudo's airlock, Zilv?"

"Only with Rotrudo's permission."

"You don't have some way you can do it without him?"

"I can enter a student's quarters only with the student's permission."

"Can't you see what's happening?"

"Yes."

He repressed a spurt of anger. He had to stay rational and alert. The Ersar-Aswero were moving with deadly, efficient co-ordination. This had been carefully planned. They had to have some plan for forcing their quarry out of the shelter of the vehicle.

Elinee pointed out the front window. He followed her arm and saw one of the flat cars disappear behind a dune. At the rear of the deck was a device he had never seen before, but whose function was obvious. Filed in front of the device were several large boulders.

"Shall we go now?" he asked. "Or shall we stay and see if it works?"

His ability to talk and think pleased his vanity. He would have made a good soldier in the old days. He was afraid of death, but his fear didn't conquer him.

"It may not be accurate," Elinee said. They had decided to stay.

A boulder rose above the dune. He followed it and for a moment it seemed to hang directly above him. He put up his hands. Elinee gasped. The boulder hit the ground just off the right wing and the wreckage on the control panel rattled.

They waited for the next shot. This was a new experience, bombardment, and Jenorden quickly discovered it was hard to endure. He wanted to bolt for the airlock. He was helpless. There was nothing he could do to stop the boulders. He turned on Zilv, "Why can't you stop this? Isn't this your world? You've got the power. Go out there and order them to stop."

"We cannot interfere."

Elinee moaned. He swung around in time to see another boulder rise above the dune. Some part of his mind tried to think of a way they could contact Rotrudo. There was a signal beside the airlock door, but Rotrudo might be a long way from a control which would open it to them. They couldn't radio him, either. While they were inside the dome, they had talked to him with the loudspeakers in their belts and they didn't know what frequency he used. Even if they had known, Rotrudo trusted the Borg and didn't wear his suit inside his dome. If he was in the lecture room, it might be hours before he heard whatever signal the airlock entrance gave off.

The boulder landed to the right and near the tail. The next one, or the one after, would land on top of them.

"Let's go," he said. "Don't use your shield too much. Save it until we're at the airlock. Keep them down with your gun."

He ran down the aisle. Zilv was still squatting on the rear seat. "Are you coming?" he yelled.

"No," Zilv said. He was looking out the window. His eye stalks were moving so much it was obvious he was observing everything.

They entered the airlock and drew their weapons. He looked at Elinee's worried face and it occurred to him she had never been in a battle before.

"You don't have to kill them," he said. "Just keep them away from us. Keep them down so they can't shoot. I'm afraid, too."

"It doesn't show."

"I've learned something. If you keep it from showing, it's easier to fight it."

The door opened. He was certain the Ersar-Aswero wanted to capture them, not kill them—only an attempt to gain information made any sense—and that meant they probably wouldn't shoot while he and Elinee were still inside the vehicle. Crouching to one side of the door, he studied the ground.

The vehicle was in a hollow surrounded by several low dunes. He knew there was a group behind the two dunes, directly in front of him, between the vehicle and the dome, to his left, in front of the vehicle, and another group behind him. There might be a group on his right, but there was some chance they hadn't had time to complete the encirclement.

He pointed right, toward the rear of the vehicle. "We'll run that way. We'll capture the nearest dune and make them come after us. We just have to hold them off until they run out of air."

"Go ahead."

He jumped out, hitting the ground in a crouch, and she landed beside him. He turned right and started running.

A crossbow bolt shot across their path. Elinee cried out and Jenorden stopped in his tracks. Twisting, he pointed his gun at the dunes. Another bolt hit the ground in front of him.

Where were they? He couldn't see a single bowman.

His inexperience overwhelmed him. He had superior weapons but the primitives were fighters and had been all their lives. The bolts were more unnerving than bullets. Bullets couldn't be seen, but the bolts were visible and they were swift, stubby and heavy.

Something flashed on the side of a dune. His reflexes brought his gun up to eye level and a bullet kicked up the dust before he had time to think.

He turned and started to run. Before be completed a stride, a bolt shot across his path.

He stopped again. He wanted to crawl into the ground. There was no cover.

He stared at the dunes. Every flash made him start. How could he keep them down with his gun when he couldn't see them?

His hand jumped to his belt. "Activate your shield! Run hard!"

A bolt ricocheted off his shield and the force field drove it into the ground at his feet. He stared at it and then he started to run. That had been aimed to hit him, not maneuver him, and it had been aimed low. They probably wanted to wound and then take prisoners.

Using up energy they would need, sooner or later, to power their guns, they ran toward the dune he had selected. Two more bolts struck his shield before the Ersar-Aswero adjusted to the new weapon and stopped shooting.

They reached the top of the dune without opposition. Three armored figures were bounding away down the other side. Jenorden raised his gun to shoot. He got one between his sights and then he lowered his arm. They looked too vulnerable. He could have killed all three of them while they were at the top of their trajectory.

They dropped to their stomachs and switched off their shields. They were both breathing hard. Glancing at an indicator on his belt, he knew he should avoid using his shield again.

They started hollowing out a depression in the sand. "How do you feel?" he asked. He couldn't see her face. He was facing the vehicle and she was facing the other way.

"Do you think we're safe now?"

"We're safer."

A bolt slid through the sand, missing his hand by a finger length. He twisted around onto his back and fired at a helmet on the dune behind him. The helmet disappeared, but he didn't know if he had hit it or not.

Too late he realized their best strategy would have been to continue running in that direction until the Ersar-Aswero didn't dare go further from their dome with their meager air supply. Now they would have to stay here and fight. If they tried to run that way now without their shields, they would be running toward three hidden crossbows. And if they tried to run it with their shields on, they might run out of energy before the Ersar-Aswero ran out of air.

"Where do they hide?" Elinee murmured.

"Between the sand grains probably. This is their whole life."

A boulder shot above the dune which hid the catapult. As soon as he saw it his fear overcame him. The boulder hit the base of their dune and he closed his eyes and buried his face in the dust.

Fearfully he raised his head. For a moment he concentrated on mastering his terror. His brain was paralyzed. Everything they could do, stay or run, looked too dangerous.

The dome airlock swung open. Three blue flashes shot from the entrance and disappeared behind the two dunes which hid the first group of Ersar-Aswero. Armored figures bounded from behind the two dunes like birds scared from cover.

Jenorden yelled. His arm shot forward, aiming at an Ersar-Aswero who was at the top of his leap, and he pulled the trigger twice. A bullet made a wide hole in the soft, primitive armor and the Ersar-Aswero dropped his crossbow and finished his trajectory as a lifeless heap which crashed to the ground chest first and lay sprawled and still on the sand.

He raised his eyes from the sights and tried to pick another target. More blue flashes shot from the airlock at the scattering primitives. For a vivid moment an armored figure glowed bright, ruddy copper against a background of stars. There were targets all over the place but again he hesitated. This wasn't like the fight with the Horta. He knew these people. He had talked to them. He knew he had to fight them if he wanted to live, that was the reality and his brain couldn't evade it, but at the same time he couldn't be indifferent when they died.

Crossbow bolts sped toward the airlock. Already the Ersar-Aswero had adjusted to the surprise attack and were hidden and returning their new adversary's fire. They seemed to have a maneuver for every contingency.

Rotrudo's huge figure appeared in the entrance. He was dressed in a transparent space suit and he was carrying a weapon proportioned to his size, a metal shield half the length of his body with a wide, stubby barrel sticking out the middle. He fired a long burst, spraying the area with blue flashes, and edged several steps away from the airlock. Setting the weapon on the ground, he crouched behind the shield.

"He's covering the front of this dune," Jenorden said. "If he stays there, they can't attack us. They'll probably turn the catapult on him, but he's making them use up time. He looks like he's figured the situation out."

Rotrudo fired a burst. A bolt struck his shield and several bolts bounced off the dome. Jenorden searched for targets. He had never realized finding something to shoot at was such an important, difficult part of fighting.

A minute passed. Rotrudo remained crouched behind his shield and the Ersar-Aswero stopped wasting bolts.

"They're probably aiming the catapult at him. He could have stayed in the airlock, but the line of fire from the airlock between those two dunes doesn't cover us."

"He's taking a terrible risk for us," Elinee said.

Jenorden glanced at an indicator on his belt. If they ran for the airlock, their converters would be exhausted before they were halfway there. He decided to remain on the dune and wait for the Ersar-Aswero to run out of air.

The catapult heaved another boulder into the sky. It started to drop and he closed his eyes again. When he opened them, the boulder was blocking the airlock entrance. Immediately another boulder rose against the stars and fell toward Rotrudo. Rotrudo watched it, calculating its trajectory, and then picked up his weapon and lumbered away from the dome.

Suddenly Ersar-Aswero exposed themselves in every direction as they bounded into new positions. Behind him Elinee fired shot after shot. Three Ersar-Aswero appeared on his left and leaped across the open space toward the dome. His gun arm stiffened and followed one of them up from the ground and fired when it was at the top of its arc. Again a wide hole appeared in the armor and the Ersar-Aswero crashed to the ground near the two he and Rotrudo had already killed.

He fired at the other two as they disappeared behind a dune. Between the two dunes he could see Rotrudo turning his weapon in a wide arc and firing continuously.

Rotrudo was trying to cover two directions at once. The Ersar-Aswero had obviously decided to eliminate him first. If they were willing to accept a few deaths their co-ordinated maneuvers could do it quickly. They could come at Rotrudo from either dune and still be protected from the humans.

Rotrudo picked up his weapon and backed between the two dunes into the central open space. Jenorden scanned the top and sides of every dune around the hollow. A new emotion was beginning to dominate his feelings. Rotrudo was risking his life for them. He had to risk his life for Rotrudo, if that was necessary.

He glanced at the dune on his left. If the Ersar-Aswero were the tacticians they appeared to be, they had to have at least one bowman hidden on the far side of that dune. He couldn't protect Rotrudo's back if he stayed where he was.

His hands loaded explosive shells into the chamber. Slipping and sliding, he ran down the face of the dune. He was exposed now and his only protection was his gun. Crouching, he fired on the run. The shell hit the far side of the dune and stirred up a gigantic, silent cloud of sand. He fired again, stirring up a cloud almost as tall as Rotrudo, and then he was at the bottom of the dune and running across the open space.

"What are you doing?" Elinee radioed.

"Protecting Rotrudo. Shoot! Keep shooting!"

Ersar-Aswero fired on him from all over the dunes in front of Rotrudo. Rotrudo raked their positions with his weapon and most of the bolts fell short or missed by yards. No one had time to take aim. Both sides were relying on fire power.

He fired another shell and plunged into the dust. The instant he rounded the dune his reflexes threw him to the ground.

In front of him an Ersar-Aswero bounded out of sight around the dune and another Ersar-Aswero shouldered a crossbow and released the catch. His finger convulsed on the trigger. A silent, invisible blow shoved the bowman back and knocked him to the ground, and the crossbow launched its bolt at the stars.

He rose to a crouch and searched for the sniper who had fled. Dropping to the ground again, he crawled around the dune.

"Jenorden! Jenorden!"

The scream jerked his head off the ground. He looked back. Ersar-Aswero were pouring over the two dunes and bounding across the open space past the wrecked vehicle. He couldn't see Rotrudo or even a single blue flash.

He stood up and ran for the next dune with strides that brought his knees up to his stomach. Rotrudo had to be dead. Even if he was only wounded, there was nothing he could do to save him from so many.

He glanced over his shoulder. The leader of the oncoming horde was landing beside the dune he had just fled. He fired several shots on the run and a bullet hit the leader square in the chest. Before the armored back hit the ground, a dozen warriors landed beside it and launched themselves into their next bound.

"Are you all right?" He was shouting. He couldn't control his voice.

"They're attacking," Elinee radioed. "They've killed Rotrudo!"

He looked back. Three of the group pursuing him had gotten far ahead of the others. Like animals pouncing on his back, they were sailing through space and aiming their crossbows as they came. "Shoot to kill!" He fired at the one in front. "Protect yourself!"

"I'm fighting them. There aren't many. They're after you." He reached a dune and crouched behind its protecting flank. Three-quarters of the *crar* were coming at him across the ground between this dune and the last one. Half a dozen of them were descending on a point just in front of his hiding place. He couldn't possibly outrun them. If he wanted to live, he had to stand here and fight.

He stood up and ran. His hand shoved his pistol into his holster. He had reached his limit. He had killed as many as he could.

He looked back. They were coming over the top and around the sides of the dune. Two more jumps and they would be all around him.

He glanced at his belt. If he turned on his shield he would be disarmed in less than a minute. His decision to die rather than fight would be irrevocable. They would capture him, and try to get information out of him, and in two or three days they would torture him to death or his suit would foul and he would die.

The next dune was a long way off. Already bolts must be speeding toward his legs. They were standing on the last dune, he didn't have to look back to know it, and now they could stand still and aim without having to duck bullets and blue flashes.

A bolt struck his shield and bounced. Bolts landed all around him, scattering as they bounced off his shield. He didn't know when what part of him had decided to activate the shield.

He jumped behind the dune. His shield winked off and he looked back and saw a line of Ersar-Aswero standing on the dune he had just left. He was helpless. Panic-stricken, he looked down and thought about digging into the sand.

He stood up and ran for the next dune. Harsh, sobbing gasps resonated inside his hood.

He made himself look back. They weren't there. They weren't pursuing him. There was no line of bowmen standing on the dune."

He stopped running. "Elinee!"

"They're leaving! They're getting on their flat cars."

"Are you all right?"

"I killed one."

He trudged across the route he had just run. As he parsed each Ersar-Aswero body, he paused long enough to make himself fully aware of what he had done.

Rotrudo was sprawled face down in the center of the open space. There was a bolt in the small of his back and another bolt between his shoulders.

Elinee stumbled off the dune. Her face and the way she walked told him everything she was feeling. She was not the same person she had been when they left Rotrudo's airlock. With one deed, the killing of an intelligent being, she had changed herself for life.

He looked from her face to Rotrudo's body. Overcome by the heavy sadness of irrevocable loss, he put his arms around her shoulders and held her against his chest. Neither of them — Rotrudo, and the Elinee who had been — would ever be with him again.

He looked at the bodies scattered on the field. He wasn't the same, either. For the second time in his life, the third counting the hunt with N. Rarkal, he had been exposed to violence and death.

Chapter 9

The vehicle landed beside the Borg dome. The airlock opened and Jenorden climbed down the ladder and trudged to the microphone station and its attendant Ivel.

"May I talk to the Borg?"

The Ivel bent his knees. "You may, but it is rarely necessary. Whatever your request, usually the Ivel can help you."

"What I have to say has to be said to the Borg."

"Many beings think that and then they request something we could have arranged. The Borg should not be disturbed unnecessarily."

"I don't have a request. I have something to say."

"You can tell me."

"Get me the Borg!"

The eye stalks regarded him. Keeping one eye on his face, the Ivel bent its other eye toward the control box it attended. One leg reached out and pressed a button.

He looked up. Far above, at least a mile, several Borg hung near the edge of the dome. He saw them through a vague shimmer, a thin atmosphere or some other medium for transmitting the sound from the loudspeaker, which had appeared as soon as the Ivel pressed the button.

"Tell us what you want to say, Jenorden."

Nothing he could see indicated their method of communication. The black shapes were just as featureless as ever.

"Do you know what happened outside Rotrudo's dome? Do you know Rotrudo's dead?"

"We know."

"Why couldn't Zilv help us? With all your power, you couldn't stop a little brawl like that one?"

"We do not interfere in the actions of other life forms."

"Wasn't it interference when you took barbarians off their own worlds and exposed them to advanced knowledge? You've interfered in the life of every intelligent being here. If it weren't for you, Rotrudo would still be alive."

"If you'll only study what we're trying to do, all your questions will be answered."

"After what happened today, I'm supposed to go back to my dome and trust you? You do something which violates moral principles every civilized being accepts. You bring races at every level together on one world—and I see people die because of it!—and then you expect me to trust you?"

"What proof can we give you?"

"Tell me why you're doing this. Explain yourselves!"

"We're trying to. We've been trying to since you got here."

"Why can't you tell me now?"

"There are some things… if you're not prepared…"

"How long will it take?"

"We can't say yet. Can't you be patient?"

It was hopeless. He could deduce the rest of the dialogue as if it were a mathematical theorem. Every time he talked to them he ended up running around the same circle.

He stalked back to the vehicle. He had come here prepared to accept part of the blame for Rotrudo's death, but now he was so angry he blamed them and only them. What intelligent being at his level of the stage of the Ersar-Aswero and the Eb wouldn't try to steal knowledge they could exploit? Normally it would have been centuries, even millennia, before the Ersar-Aswero left their planet. A world like this was bound to cause trouble. And to set up such a world, to encourage beings to come here and then not take reasonable precautions, to claim you couldn't interfere, to give every being perfect freedom of the planet—that was the irresponsibility of madness!

Roseka met him at the airlock of their dome. Elinee had been drugged and asleep for the last hour.

"What did they say?"

He scowled. "What they always say. They can't interfere. Be patient, everything will be explained. Let's go! Why waste our time? I'm not going to stay here for the next decade, hoping they'll explain themselves someday. And after today I'm not going to prowl around causing trouble, either."

"You've been through a terrible shock. Wait awhile. You don't want to leave here any more than I do."

"There are races in the galaxy no human has ever heard of which have just as much to teach us as the Borg, and don't hide themselves behind a lot of mystery."

"I can't agree with you. The Borg could be the biggest discovery in human history. I've sat through lectures which make a few days on this world worth months of visiting other worlds. What I've learned about the psychology of intelligent races no one on Earth has even approached."

"Assuming what they're teaching you is true."

"If it isn't, they have fantastically detailed imaginations."

"How long are you willing to give them?"

"A few more months, at least that. After that we'll have to decide if it's worth staying. Right now it's too early to decide." Strong emotions surged across her face. "I can't leave here now. This may be the only real chance to deal with the Horta I'll ever have. It would torment me the rest of my life if I left here now."

That couldn't be argued with.

The next day was his turn to guard the ship. He slept fitfully, and when he reached the ship he felt tired and restless at the same time. He couldn't seem to do anything more than a few minutes. He would pick up his instrument and then in the middle of a song put it down and dive into the pool. A minute later he would climb out of the water and stand by the window looking at the stars.

Sometimes while he was standing there the ship passed over the Borg dome. Every time he saw it, he understood why the founders of the human community had been profoundly disturbed when scientists developed the interstellar drive. The unknown was a source of danger. Contacts with unpredictably different races could arouse dangerous emotions. If men learned to hate again among the stars, the young, still developing peace created on Earth might be destroyed before it was a century old.

Chapter 10

Crouching back to back with N. Rarkal, Jenorden watched the grass and tried to ignore the reactions of his glands and nerves. There were two herkan loose in the field and N. Rarkal had made it vividly clear two were several times more dangerous than one. According to her they would probably attack simultaneously from one direction, forcing one hunter to turn around and aim in the brief interval he had been given last time just for aiming. So far, after several wearing minutes, they had seen no sign of either animal.

"We may not get any warning," N. Rarkal said. "Stay alert. They may crawl until they're close enough to jump."

"Is this their worst maneuver?"

"I think it is."

"How often do they do it?"

"Almost every time. When we hunt three, usually two attack together and one attacks from the opposite direction."

Elinee was standing on the wall. She had wanted to hunt with them, for the experience, and then at the last minute she had decided she couldn't.

She was standing by herself. Nolten had retired to his personal dwelling soon after he had helped N. Rarkal welcome them. N. Rarkal said Nolten now spent most of his time in his dwelling, enjoying some pleasure, apparently a story-telling device, he had brought with him from home. The device was popular, even encouraged, in the culture of the Togme of Bel, and Nolten could use it for unlimited periods for the first time in his life. Enforced idleness, and being light years from home and authority, seemed to be eroding Nolten's character.

As for Emcasa, he and his pressurized tractor had both disappeared from the dome yesterday morning. N. Rarkal had greeted them with her usual courtesy, but Jenorden knew she was shaken. She was not as nonchalant about killing a member of her own species as she had appeared to be. She had mentioned Emcasa's disappearance several times as they drove to the hunting ground, and it was obvious she was looking for an excuse not to kill him.

The grass bent in the wind. The dark vegetation and the cold light made Jenorden think of an autumn afternoon on Earth. The air, if he could have breathed it, would have been chilly and stimulating.

After the battle with the Ersar-Aswero, he had thought he would never want to face danger again. But the days had passed — it had now been an Earth month since Rotrudo's death — and he had grown increasingly restless and dissatisfied with what he was doing. He had hiked, and loafed on the ship, and even wasted a few hours a day in the Borg lecture room, but all the while he had felt as if there was some¬thing he was not doing. As soon as N. Rarkal had called and mentioned hunting, he had known what he wanted. He wanted to look death in the eye again. His consciousness of death was slowly destroying him, and he had been educated to face his problems, not evade them.

N. Rarkal yelled. He heard the wild shriek of a herkan, and the rustle of a great body lifting itself from the grass, and he whirled. Both animals were hurtling through the air at them. N. Rarkal was already aiming, fierce, short noises breaking from her throat.

She was firing at the herkan on the right. The other one was leaping at him. Bending his arm at the wrist and the elbow, he leveled his gun. His face was a complicated system of tensions. Every emotion in his body was focused on the oncoming danger.

His gun roared. The herkan's face became a mess of brains and blood and gore and the body hurled over his bent back and landed in the grass.

They looked at their kill and then at each other. Relief and a strange affection flooded his being. She had stood between him and death. She and only she. The last hunt had been exciting, but this one had evoked a deeper emotion.

He was certain her eyes were expressing a similar feeling. He thought he understood the function hunting had in her culture.

"When your people quarrel," he said, "what do they do?"

"They hunt together."

"That's what I thought."

"Does it seem strange to you?"

"It works. It does what it's supposed to do."

"Thank you." She stared at him a moment longer and then she gestured at the two herkan. "They're beautiful creatures, but we think we sacrifice them to a good cause."

They cleared the grass around the bodies. Together they lit the fires and watched the animals bum.

They walked to the wall in silence. Jenorden felt pleased with himself. He had acquired a piece of knowledge, an insight into another culture, which the community would not have obtained if he had merely studied the Eb from the outside.

This might even be an institution the community could use. If machines could be substituted for living creatures, hunting might be a useful addition to the community's peacekeeping techniques. Or would it tend to intensify the appetite for destruction? He wasn't sure. A culture devoted to the fulfillment of life might need the occasional shock of violent death. Otherwise it might forget what it was fighting and its rituals and ceremonies might become meaningless. "I keep wondering what you're thinking," N. Rarkal said.

"If I could tell you, you'd be pleased."

"Are you trying to comfort me?"

"I'm telling you the truth. After what we've just done together, don't you believe me?"

"After what we've just done, I have to. Thank you."

Elinee put down the ladder and they climbed over the wall and walked to N. Rarkal's car. Elinee was pensive. As they rode back to the Eb dwelling, her thoughtful face told him she still felt disturbed because she hadn't participated in the hunt. He did his best to show her it was all right.

He leaned forward, putting his head next to N. Rarkal's shoulder. "How can one person hunt three of those things alone?"

N. Rarkal turned her head. "Very few can. You have to be fast and you have to be clever."

"I don't think I could watch it," Elinee said.

"I've seen crowds of spectators drop on all fours with excitement."

N. Rarkal turned back to the road. As they rounded the curve, he saw Emcasa's pressurized tractor blocking the road, and at the same time he heard two sharp cracks. N. Rarkal threw up her arms, blood gushing from her skull. Elinee screamed. N. Rarkal slumped over the wheel and the car swerved off the road into the side of the hill.

Jenorden lunged at the steering wheel. Without really knowing what was happening, reacting before his mind could adjust to the sudden, shocking event, he steered them along the side of the hill. The car lurched to a halt and they dove behind it and drew their weapons. An automatic weapon chattered at them from the trees. The back of the tractor had opened up and Ersar-Aswero were pouring out. Bullets cracked above their heads.

They were both stunned by horror. Emcasa had killed a member of his own species. N. Rarkal's blood was smeared on Jenorden's sleeves.

The Ersar-Aswero were bounding toward them. He glanced at Elinee and the two of them stood up and ran for the bend in the road.

A bolt shot past his legs. He turned and snapped a pair of shots as he ran. The Ersar-Aswero were gaining on them fast. Their suits encumbered them less in this environment than they had in the airless wasteland.

They rounded the turn. They were still only a short distance from the hunting field and the building where the herkan were caged. On their left, about half a mile from the road, there was a small wood.

"Head for the trees! We'll hide in the trees!"

Elinee was already several feet ahead of him. She gestured to let him know she'd heard and they both turned off the road toward the woods. Behind them Ersar-Aswero came around the turn and over the hill. Bolts shot past him at chest level and he realized they were willing to kill him after all.

He hit the grass. Feverishly he snapped half a dozen incendiaries into his pistol. He felt as if he were stuck in one of those recurrent dreams some people had. How long would it take him to reach his limit this time? Already he could feel an insistent urge to switch on his shield and run for the woods. But that would be folly. This time they not only had him outnumbered, they had as much time as they needed. If Emcasa had transported his allies between the domes in his tractor, he must have brought a good supply of their atmosphere with him. As long as he had his gun, he could at least shoot to scare them, even if he soon reached the point at which he couldn't actually kill them.

He fired the incendiaries and the grass lit with a roar. Tall flames and heavy white smoke shielded him from the Ersar-Aswero onslaught.

A group of them bounced into sight on his right, bypassing the wall of smoke and intent on Elinee. They held their crossbows diagonally across their chest and their bodies were perfectly motionless. Only their legs moved, bending as they came down and straightening the instant they hit.

He fired at the grass in front of them and they sailed through a wall of fire and smoke which shot up almost the instant he pulled the trigger. He turned around just as a warrior, crossbow aimed, sailed through the first wall of smoke. He fired at the hard, armored chest and the incendiary struck home and turned the armor into an oven.

He turned around. Through the thin mist of smoke from his second barrage, he could see Elinee running and the Ersar-Aswero dropping on her back.

He raised his gun and aimed at the leader. He wanted to face both directions at once. They were probably falling on his back at the same time they were falling on hers.

"Shoot! Turn around and shoot!"

He fired. Elinee turned, bringing her weapon up, and the first warrior to hit the ground got Jenorden's bullet in his back. The others landed, crossbows ready, and there was a quick, violent scuffle. Elinee's gun was knocked from her hand. Two Ersar-Aswero grabbed her shoulders and leaped toward the hill and the tractor. She struggled with them, kicking and thrashing even when they were at the top of their trajectory and she could have dropped several yards into the flames.

Jenorden dropped. Bolts flew at him through the smoke. The smoke was thinning out and he could see them bounding back to the tractor.

He stood up. Switching on his shield, he ran toward the hill.

He ran around the bend and jumped into the middle of the road. The rear door was already shut and all the Ersar-Aswero were inside. Only a crippling explosive could keep them from leaving the dome with their prisoner.

On top of the tractor the gun turret swung his way. Confronted with the bore of a small cannon, he panicked and threw himself flat in the grass. The cannon roared and a shell bigger than anything his shield could stop screamed down the road.

He crawled behind the hill. Out on the road the gun roared twice. The first shell exploded close enough to shower dirt and shrapnel on his back. The second shell whistled in a different direction. Raising his head, he followed the sound and watched it explode in the building where the herkan were caged.

Chapter 11

Stars glittered above the dome. Huddling on the narrow branch of a tree, the rough trunk pressing his spine, he stared at the thousands of glittering lights and struggled with the vision of the Horta: In the morning he had to go out on the grass and fight the hungry animals who were prowling the dark in search of their prey.

N. Rarkal was a thing, a lump of flesh. By now she was covered with vermin or her body was fueling a prowling herkan. Someday he would be a thing, too. It could happen tomorrow or it could happen in two hundred and thirty-seven years. In the time scale of the universe it didn't matter. One swift, violent moment and the passion and achievement of intelligent life were ended forever.

He could live in his suit up to four days. If he stayed in the tree he would probably outlast the herkan. There was a good chance they would be dead, or too weak to fight, before his suit turned foul and poisonous. All he had to do was huddle here. He didn't have to struggle or defy his fate.

By that time, of course, Elinee would be beyond help. Even now the tractor was crawling across the planet to the Ersar-Aswero dome. He couldn't take on the herkan in the dark, but if he came down from the tree as soon as the first mist left the ground, there was a chance he could fight his way to the airlock and get to the Ersar-Aswero dome before Emcasa.

His despair was overpowering. Let the galaxy turn without him. But this concerned someone else, another human, and his education had been long and successful. His concern for Elinee was as powerful and as irresistible as an instinct.

"Jenorden. Elinee." Roseka's voice murmured in his earphones.

He had heard her calling earlier in the evening, but his transmitter was too weak for him to answer. He was at least twenty miles from the airlock and he would have to be within five miles of her receiver before she could hear him. "I'm still here. I guess you're too far away to answer—I hope that's why you didn't answer—but if you're still alive, I'm here. I asked Zilv to open the dome and he refused. I tried to blast my way in but the shells just go right into the dome. It absorbs them. I know I told you this before, but I don't know if you heard me. I'm still here. Don't give up. I'll be here when you come out."

He switched off the receiver and closed his eyes. Knowing he had to do it, for tomorrow he had to be alert, he pushed all the terrifying knowledge from his brain, consciously relaxed his muscles, and fell into a fitful, uncomfortable sleep.

The sun which stirred him from his dreams was cold and gloomy. For almost the first time in his life, he didn't want to wake up.

He scanned the grass with his binoculars. Far away, almost on the horizon, he spotted a ripple. He was certain at least six of them were loose in the dome. Last night he had reached the tree just as they started leaping from the building.

His stomach felt sick. When he raised his binoculars again, he spotted two more ripples. He closed his eyes. His conscience was as real as the fear pounding in his temples. They had taught him what was right, and they had taught him why it was right, and he had learned the lesson willingly. And now all the terror in the universe couldn't erase the lesson from his being.

He picked his way downward through the branches of the tree. On the last thick branch, an easy hop from the ground, he hesitated again. His eyes took in the sky, and the horizon, and the cold sun shining through the dome. Drawing his gun, he stepped off the branch.

He walked toward the road. His eyes scanned the grass systematically. He wanted to run, but he knew if he did he would be worn out long before he was safe. He had to meet them in battle and kill them. That was his only chance.

He froze. Three ripples were coming his way. Two were racing toward him side by side and the third was intersecting their path at an angle.

When they were all within six hundred yards, two of them started circling and the third disappeared. He turned with the two circlers, his back tingling and his eyes searching for some sign of the other one. His hands were steady but inside he felt sick and trembling. The circlers were getting further apart. Already the front one was almost half a turn ahead of the other.

They made one full turn and then a second. He had trouble keeping both of them in sight at once. He had to keep turning his head to make sure the third one wasn't attacking him from behind.

He wondered if they were intelligent enough to know they were wearing down his nerves. They had done something like this both the times he had hunted with N. Rarkal. Or were they just afraid, as he was afraid, and hesitating until the needs of their bodies drove them toward food? They were doing what they had been bred to do, and he was doing what he had been educated to do.

He looked behind him and saw the ripple streaking at his back. He whirled and the other two broke from their circle and charged.

He didn't wait for it to leap. As it reached the point where it would normally spring, his gun roared and an explosive shell smashed into the oncoming ripple. The ground shook. Dirt and grass and flesh fountained into the air and he turned just as the other two leaped. His first shell grazed a winged side, exploding and knocking the wounded body off course, and he turned on the third animal and shot it in the face when it was only a few feet from his own fear-contorted features. The shell penetrated the body before it went off, and the muffled explosion shoved him to the ground as he tried to back away.

He picked up his gun and stood up. In the grass the herkan he had wounded was screaming and thrashing as it died. The other two had been blown to pieces. Drained of emotion, exhausted by an instant of fear and action, he stared dully at the tortured body. He wanted to end its pain, but he didn't want to use up an explosive shell and he didn't want to stop long enough to switch to regular ammunition. He tried to think, and then he turned his back on the wounded animal and trudged toward the road.

A herkan leaped from the grass. There was no ripple, no warning of any kind except the rush of a massive body lifting itself off the ground. He screamed and brought up his gun and his finger convulsed on the trigger. Wings beat and claws and teeth sped toward his face. The gun roared in his hand. A strange swelling appeared in the middle of the animal's body. He dropped to one knee, throwing up his left hand. The front half of the body sailed over his head and the gory mess of the rear half crashed to the ground beside him.

He stood up and stumbled away from the carcass. In the open, a good quarter mile from the bodies and the torn up ground, he stopped and waited for the next attack. The herkan he had wounded was still screaming.

From the far end of the dome three ripples converged on him as relentlessly as if they were missiles placed in a trajectory and lacked any will of their own. Under the grass, only inches from the ground, their heads were raised to catch the scent and their claws were sheathing and unsheathing with excitement.

Crouching, he held his gun with relaxed fingers and awaited their attack. They had passed the wall and were moving parallel to the road less than a mile away. They would break from the grass in a few seconds.

They split apart. One turned right and the other left and the middle one charged him head on. He sighted on the middle one and the ripple on the left slid out of his peripheral vision.

Almost simultaneously herkan sprang at him from the front and from the right. He pressed the trigger and shot the first one as it cleared the grass and then he turned on the second and fired again. The hasty shot hit it near the tail and knocked it off course. As it flew past him its wings struck his shoulders and knocked him to the ground. He landed on all fours, scrambling for balance, and the third herkan leaped at him at close range.

He snapped a shot. The thing kept coming. The bullet had hit but it had missed the face and it hadn't been an explosive. He fired again and threw himself forward, under the oncoming body and away from the head. The heavy stomach landed on his ribs. Legs kicked his chest and wings beat on his face through his suit. He fired twice, directly into the belly, as the herkan thrashed and tried to reach him with its fangs. Blood gushed from the bullet holes. The animal screamed and bucked and he kicked himself out from under and fired at its head. His arms and the lower half of his body were covered with blood.

He stood up. Two clouded eyes stared at him, and then the herkan dropped its head and died.

The herkan he had wounded in the tail sprang from the grass. He screamed and a rush of surprise and horror made him throw up his left hand and stumble back.

His right hand did what it was trained to do. The bullet hit the herkan square in the head and he threw himself down. Long after the body hit the ground, he lay on the grass and stared at his hands.

Chapter 12

Roseka followed Emcasa's tracks all the way to the Ersar-Aswero dome. She didn't admit she was too late until she saw the tracks ending at the closed airlock.

She returned to the Eb dome and picked up Jenorden. As they flew to their dome, they radioed the ship and told Veneleo what had happened.

Veneleo was stunned. "As soon as we get to our dome," Roseka said, "we're going to call Emcasa. If that doesn't work, we'll talk to the Borg."

"Do you think they'll help?" Veneleo asked.

"They have to."

"They don't interfere."

"Even they can't be that indifferent."

"Don't make me wait for news. Tell me as soon as something happens."

"We'll call you as often as we can," Roseka said.

"If she dies…" The words trailed off.

They called Emcasa as soon as they reached their dome. "You're alive, Jenorden. I'm glad. I was afraid those beasts might kill you. I'm sorry I had to delay you that way."

"Elinee can't give you any information, Emcasa. None of us can. When something is this immoral to us, it's impossible."

"Why is it immoral? You can't make things any worse for us than they are. Do you think I'd do what I've done if that wasn't true? Do you think I'm a murderer because I like it?"

"The prohibition is absolute. I can't do what you want me to do."

"I don't believe you."

"You'll kill her — you'll murder someone else — and you'll learn nothing."

"You can be the saviors of a world. Doesn't that mean anything to you? Is our fate so petty to you you can't care?"

"We do care," Roseka said. "That's why our teachers taught us so well nothing that happens can change us. They knew we'd be tempted."

Emcasa's big eyes studied them. "How can I know you're telling the truth? I have to test you. If you're lying, you'll give me what I want before she dies. I'm sorry. What else can I do?" Jenorden had learned enough about Eb expressions to know he was truly in agony. "Jenorden, I'm sorry! If you're telling the truth, forgive me! I've done too much. I can't stop now."

"She'll die, Emcasa. We aren't lying."

"I almost believe you. Call me if you decide you can save her."

The screen blanked. "She's going to die!" Roseka whispered.

He stalked toward the door. Roseka watched him go and then she started after him. He piloted the vehicle a short distance from the Borg dome and this time the attendant didn't argue with him. The Borg appeared as soon as he demanded their presence.

"You know what's happened," he said. "You must. Will you help us?"

"We can't," the loudspeaker said. "We want to, Jenorden, but we can't. We have our morality, too."

He stared at the high dome and the black shapes a mile above his head. They were telling him the same thing he had told Emcasa, and he didn't believe them any more than Emcasa had believed him. How could he believe Elinee was doomed?

"At least let us into that dome so we can fight for her!"

"We can't. Once we give any being a dome, only he can open it."

He clenched his fists. If he had been a little less rational, he would have drawn his gun and vented his anger by shooting at the dome. What kind of beings were they?

"We're sorry. We didn't want this to happen."

He turned away. Two hours later he dove on the Ersar-Aswero dome.

Shell after shell poured out of the cannon at the airlock. Most of them were direct hits. A few hit the side of the dome. All were absorbed exactly as Roseka had said they would be.

He turned around and flew back to their dome. Neither of them had the strength to radio Veneleo.

When they entered the house, he went straight to the screen and called Emcasa. This time the Eb took his time coming.

"What are you going to do?" Roseka asked.

"Talk. Just talk. What else can I do? At least as long as we're talking, I can hope."

Emcasa appeared on the screen. "Have you decided to help us, Jenorden?"

"What can we do to convince you we can't?"

"You can let Elinee die."

"Is that all you have to say?"

"Can you think of anything else?"

"If we give you any information, will the Ersar-Aswero get it, too?"

"You're bargaining?"

"I'm asking for information. The more I know, the more chance there is I can think of a way out of this."

"We'll discuss it when you're ready to bargain. When you have something to say, call me."

The screen blanked and Jenorden shut it off with a blow. Roseka couldn't look at him. His anguish looked like something no human nervous system could endure.

He turned away from the screen. Then his face softened. He felt the first stirring of the same fear he had felt that morning, the terror of doing something he was afraid to do and yet was forced to do by his own irresistible drives. He turned back to the screen and watched his hands manipulate the controls.

Three Ersar-Aswero appeared on the screen and began their elaborate greeting ceremonies. Deliberately, insultingly, he interrupted them.

"You're all cowards." Haltingly, choosing his words carefully, he spoke as well as he could in their language. All primitives were different, but the Ersar-Aswero were warriors, and warrior primitives usually had a strong sense of honor. "You took Elinee by ambush. You're afraid to meet us in open combat. You learned to fear me the first time we fought. When I leave this world, I'm going to spread your shame to every planet in the galaxy. Your race will be ashamed to leave its native world. You aren't a *crar*. A *crar* has morals. You're a pack of unorganized, nameless animals."

He turned off the screen. When he glanced at Roseka, she nodded her approval. "Good thinking, Jenorden."

"You know what this means if it works? If I could have kept myself from doing it, I would have."

"I know."

"It may not work."

"Do you think you can fight them? After this morning, after what you went through in the Eb dome..."

"I don't know what I can do. I'll find out when the time comes."

A long time passed. Outside the sun set and insects and small animals began making night noises. The house was silent. Roseka lay on her bed and he lay on his. Neither of them felt like talking.

The Ersar-Aswero would be fighting in their own environment and Emcasa would have the heavy weapons mounted on his tractor. It would be worse than anything he had endured that morning.

Until he had made the call he had been moral and high-minded and suffering for Elinee. Now he was once again faced with the possibility he might die. Worry about others and worry about oneself were not the same emotion.

The screen buzzed. He rolled out of bed and walked to the common room.

Roseka got to the screen before him. She turned it on and Emcasa appeared and touched horns.

"I've been talking to my colleagues. They think you should come here if you want to talk. We've decided face-to-face discussions might be useful."

Jenorden's heart jumped. Concealing his excitement, he looked at Emcasa scornfully. "So you can take another prisoner?"

"I already have the only prisoner I need. You may come with your usual weapons. The Ersar-Aswero will meet you at the airlock." Emcasa paused. "They're the ones that want this."

"Why can't we talk now?"

"The Ersar-Aswero feel uncomfortable negotiating over long distances. They aren't used to modern communications. This doesn't seem real to them."

"Suppose we come tomorrow morning? Does that suit you?"

"I'll tell the Ersar-Aswero you're coming. Elinee isn't hurt, by the way. She's guarded, but we aren't torturing her."

Jenorden bowed. "Thank you. I'm certain you aren't cruel."

"I have my morality, too."

The screen blanked and he turned to Roseka. Her emotions were just as mixed as his. He put his arms around her and they took what comfort they could from the touch of bodies encased in suits.

"He's still pretending we're coming for a conference," Roseka said.

"He's probably leaving it up to us. They'll be ready for a fight but we can back down if we want to. Let's call Veneleo."

Veneleo had his moment of jubilation when they told him the news, and then he, too, began to think about the danger. "Do you have any clever strategies, Jenorden? You've done more fighting than any of us."

"I've got a few ideas, but nothing we can do will make it easy. Whatever we do, it's going to be bloody."

"It's Roseka's turn to guard the ship, isn't it?"

They both turned to Roseka. For a brief instant her face betrayed her relief, and then she regained her composure. "I'm going with Jenorden," she said.

"You're saying that," Veneleo said, "because you think you have to."

"I didn't say I want to go. I said I'm going."

"Why should you go with him?"

"Because the decision has to be made as impersonally as possible. The one who stays will feel guilty and the one who goes—his emotions won't be pleasant either. We set up the schedule for watching the ship when we first got here. It's as impersonal as any system."

"Tomorrow is Jenorden's day."

Jenorden felt irritated. They were indulging in a luxury. Veneleo was right. They both felt obliged to offer and neither of them could afford to withdraw. Withdrawal would be psychologically damaging. He glanced around the room. In the pre-community days humans had rolled dice and flipped coins. Money and games of chance were both obsolete, but there must be something he could use.

He took a bullet from his belt. "Let this settle it." Squatting he laid the bullet on the floor and flipped it with his finger. Veneleo and Roseka watched it spin with fascinated eyes. It slowed, and then it stopped, and after a while he lifted his head and looked at the screen.

Veneleo nodded. He didn't try to pretend he was unconcerned.

Roseka looked relieved and then she looked at Veneleo and her eyes grew sad. "I'm not happy either."

"I believe you," Veneleo said.

The carefree look had left Veneleo's face. His love of life and happiness, an emotion all humans honored and respected, was too great for him to face death stoically.

"I'm sorry," Jenorden said. "I'm sorry, Veneleo. If I could do this by myself, I would."

"Don't blame yourself. You've only done what you had to do. You're right, if anybody's to blame, it's the Borg."

Roseka touched Jenorden's arm. He turned to her and she looked at him questioningly. "I'm going to the ship now," she said. "Veneleo can come down in the morning."

He nodded. He wanted her, too, but they both knew Veneleo needed her more.

Chapter 13

It had to be a battle of attrition. Jenorden thought about it, brooding as he stared out the window at the Borg dome, and then he discussed it with Veneleo and Roseka and they both reluctantly agreed he was right. From the moment they entered the dome, they would have to concentrate on equalizing the odds by tailing the Ersar-Aswero.

Neither of them asked how many they could kill. There would be two of them, and they were fighting for the life of another human, and they didn't feel responsible, so there was no way they could know when their revulsion would overcome their instinct to survive. They could only hope that sometime before that, the Ersar-Aswero and Emcasa would stop fighting. Surely even primitives would be revolted by so much slaughter.

For the second night in a row he was waiting for a morning which might be his last. He wondered what would happen to him tomorrow if he survived. He knew he was still functioning only because another human needed him. He had looked at death, and every day the vision planted in his psyche by the Horta grew more powerful, and tomorrow more deaths would be embedded in his consciousness.

In the morning Veneleo arrived with a fresh converter and a double supply of ammunition for him. They flew toward the north with him piloting and Veneleo sitting behind him.

He landed them several hundred yards from the Ersar-Aswero airlock, behind a dune which would protect them from any sudden attacks. Switching on the radio, he contacted Emcasa.

"Welcome, Jenorden. Welcome, Veneleo."

"Good morning, Emcasa. We'll be outside your airlock in a few minutes."

"It will open as soon as you get there. The Ersar-Aswero are waiting for you."

They stood up. Veneleo stared gloomily at the dome and then he struggled and made his face look a little like his old self.

"Are you ready?" Jenorden asked.

"Let's go."

The airlock door opened when they were still several paces from the dome. They stopped, and their fingers closed around their weapons, but the airlock was empty.

"We have to go in," Jenorden muttered. "We shouldn't take too long."

They entered the airlock and the heavy door closed behind them. Machinery hummed. Radiation sterilized their suits and the lighting dimmed to the twilight of the Ersar-Aswero environment.

They drew their weapons. In the dimness a pink light blinked three times. The inner door swung open.

They didn't stop to look things over. They had picked their strategy and ruthless as it was they had to go through with it. Jenorden fired twice, the noise of the gun reverberating in the lock and creating new pressures on his ear drums, and two explosive shells tore up the ground in front of the door. Veneleo fired an instant later and two incendiaries combined with the sparse vegetation and the powerful, constant wind of the Ersar-Aswero world to create a sheet of flame which flared toward the sky and collapsed at once.

Bolts clattered on the walls of the airlock. Jenorden threw himself flat and again two explosive shells rocked the ground. Rising, he sprinted through the dust and smoke, firing blindly and trying to create enough havoc to keep the Ersar-Aswero down. Veneleo followed on his heels.

The Ersar-Aswero had formed a semi-circle around the airlock and were shooting at them from behind the rocks and hills and out of the gullies of their rugged environment. Several warriors, incredibly, were drawn up in formation on his left and taking careful, formal aim with their crossbows. Hitting the ground as a flock of bolts flew over his back, he shot an explosive at them. The wind diverted the bullet and it exploded on their right flank and scattered the formation. In their own environment they moved even faster than they had in the

Eb dome. Here they could even ride on the wind.

He stood up and ran on. Hurdling a fallen warrior, he switched on his shield. Together he and Veneleo charged up a hill into a shower of bolts. They reached the top and went down the other side firing at the fleeing warriors. Jenorden switched off his shield as he ran.

They jumped into a gully, a natural chest-high trench. Veneleo blasted the top of the hill they had just left and they looked around for their adversaries. None were in sight. Remembering the first time he had fought them, Jenorden shuddered and peered into every shadow.

"This light," Veneleo muttered.

The wind pressure pushing on Jenorden's cheek increased drastically. Automatically he glanced down the gully.

"Duck!"

They squatted and a rock half the size of a man's fist shot over their heads. Jenorden stared sickly at the side of the gully. He could have been brained.

Veneleo fired and the sound jerked him erect. Several Ersar-Aswero were bounding over the top of the hill. He snapped a shot and then ducked as a volley of bolts sped toward the gully. When he raised his head the Ersar-Aswero were bouncing off the side of the hill and aiming a second volley as they descended on him. He snapped another shot and ducked again. In a second they would be over the trench.

The gully made a ragged semi-circle around the base of the hill. They both came to the same conclusion and ran for cover in opposite directions. Crouching behind the bend, he fired at the first Ersar-Aswero to cross the trench. The shot hit the armored warrior square in the chest. Another warrior sailed across the trench right behind the first one and Jenorden ducked a bolt and looked around the bend just in time to duck another bolt.

He looked again. They had all disappeared. Raising his head and eyes above the top of the trench, he scanned the darkness.

"Are you all right?" Veneleo radioed.

"I killed another one. I think we've killed four." The callousness of his language disgusted him, but he refused to use euphemisms.

"Watch the hill!" Veneleo yelled.

Another group, as big as the last bunch, poured over the side of the hill. Bolts flew and he caught them on his shield and then switched the shield off and shot back. Explosives tore up the hillside. Yelling battle cries and ignoring their dead, the warriors leaped toward him through the wreckage.

Turning on his shield, he surrendered the position and bolted around the hill and up another gully. He switched off his shield and turned around. They weren't following him. Trying to look up, back and ahead at the same time, he felt his way backward. His eyes ached with the effort to see in this light.

"They've disappeared," Veneleo said.

"Where are you? I'm backing up a gulley in front of the hill."

"I'm in some boulders to your left. I had to turn my shield on."

"So did I. We'd better watch our indicators."

"What do you think they'll do now?"

"Look out for ambushes. They've probably been trying to separate us. Now that they've done it, I don't think they'll make any frontal attacks. Try to keep moving further into the dome."

Through the twilight and the craggy land, they stalked the Ersar-Aswero and the Ersar-Aswero stalked them. Jenorden butchered them as methodically as if he were a slaughter machine. Only during lulls, lying in hiding while he waited for them, did he feel bitter misery.

When Veneleo shot their eighth victim, they had been inside the dome almost an hour. He had no idea where Veneleo was, except that he was far away, and he guessed he himself had moved a couple of miles into the dome. He was lying behind a boulder, resting as he worked his way up a ridge. It had been several minutes since an Ersar-Aswero had shot at him. He knew there were several of them spread out below, stalking him up the ridge, but they seemed to be resting, too.

A faint sound attracted his attention. He strained his ears.

The sound was a long way off and would have been inaudible if the wind hadn't carried it.

"Veneleo! I think I hear the tractor!"

"Can you see it?"

"Wait." He listened again. She had to be on it. Emcasa wouldn't let her out of his custody. "He's on the other side of this ridge. He's coming this way. The Ersar-Aswero must have called for help."

A scream pierced Jenorden's ear drums. "Veneleo!" Shock blurred his vision. He almost stood up and exposed himself to the Ersar-Aswero crossbows.

"Veneleo!"

Veneleo groaned. "I'm hit. Jenorden, I'm hit!"

Jenorden closed his eyes. He didn't even know where Veneleo was.

"Where? Where are you hit?"

Veneleo groaned. "My thigh… my forearm… I think my leg's… broken… ." He groaned again. Jenorden tried to think. The tractor sounded closer.

"Can you hold them off? Are you in a good position?"

"Go after Elinee."

"Can you hold them off?"

Veneleo gasped. Jenorden listened to Veneleo's quick, panting breaths rise to a crescendo of agony and he felt as if the pain were his.

"It'll take… two of… you to move me."

"Hold on. Hold them off. Don't give in."

In a sitting position, kicking himself backward with his legs, he backed away from the boulder and up the side of the ridge. Between Veneleo's groans and the sound of the oncoming tractor, he was almost in a state of panic himself. Veneleo must not die. No person so alive should die.

He sent two shells down the slope. They exploded and threw up a screen of dirt and he stood up and ran for the top of the ridge. As he went down the other side, the Ersar-Aswero leaped from their hiding places and bounded after him.

The ridge sloped downward a couple of hundred yards and then the ground sloped upward again to the back of a higher ridge. On his left, about half a mile away, there was a U-shaped opening in the opposite ridge. Emcasa's tractor was just creeping through the opening.

The automatic weapon on the tractor opened up on him and he dropped into a narrow gully, turning sideways so he could squeeze in and slipping on a floor of loose rocks. Adrenalin flooded his body. Again his fear was driving him forward.

Up the slope of the valley the tractor halted next to a group of spear-shaped rocks. Running from boulder to boulder and gully to gully, crawling on the ground with some minor upheaval in the landscape for protection and then sprinting from a place where he hoped Emcasa didn't expect him to appear, he fought his way toward it. Sometimes Emcasa fired on him with the automatic weapon and sometimes the cannon turned his way and explosive shells screamed down the valley. Behind him the Ersar-Aswero sniped at his back and drew the noose tighter. In spite of his fears he kept his shield turned off. There was plenty of cover and the light was as hard on Emcasa's marksmanship as it was on his.

He squatted in a shallow gully as close to the tractor as he wanted to get. Nervously he raised his head. The gun turret swung on him and he dropped to all fours and crawled along the gully.

"Elinee! If you're in the tractor, tell me what part. Say front or rear. One word. They won't kill you. You're too valuable."

He waited. He couldn't shoot until he knew. He couldn't see the Ersar-Aswero but he knew they were moving in on three sides. "Hurry! Hurry! It's our only chance." Even as he crouched here, pinned below ground level by the tractor's guns, they might be making their final assault.

"Front."

The sound was only a mumble, hardly a word at all, but he was certain he had heard it. "Front! I heard you. Keep still. Get ready to run."

He rose as far out of the gully as he dared. His gun came up and he sighted on the rear half of the tractor. Ersar-Aswero battle cries rang in his ears. The turret turned on him, the automatic chattering.

He squeezed the trigger and dropped. Bullets cracked above his back. An explosion shook the ground.

He raised his head. There was a gaping hole in the rear of the tractor. Ersar-Aswero were leaping toward him across the rocks. A figure in a human spacesuit was stumbling out the back of the wrecked vehicle.

He switched on his shield and stood up. In one swift, chaotic glance he saw the Ersar-Aswero charging him from three directions, Elinee stumbling across the treacherous ground with her hands tied behind her back, and the turret edging the cannon his way. Bolts ricocheted off his shield. He fired at the turret, directly at the cannon, and then he turned on the Ersar-Aswero.

He fired a barrage at the oncoming warriors. Behind him, one more sound in the din, the shell he had fired at the turret exploded against metal. Shells tore up and ground smashed into armor. Battle cries turned into death yells in midbreath.

The charge broke. The Ersar-Aswero leaped for cover and he turned on the tractor again. Emcasa was stumbling toward the rocks in his cumbersome space suit. Elinee had reached a gully and was dropping into hiding.

Switching off his shield, he dropped and crawled along his own gully. He jumped up and sprinted toward Elinee. As he ran, a line of bullets kicked up the dust behind his heels. Emcasa had another weapon.

He dropped into the gully and yelled when he realized how deep it was. Elinee was crouching at the bottom rubbing her bonds against the rocks. He broke his fall and came up ready to shoot whoever looked over the rim.

"She's free! Hold on. We're coming!"

"Is she all right?" Veneleo whispered.

He looked at her. Her eyes were filled with tears. "You came," she said. "You came." She stood up and he struggled with the knots on her bonds. "What's wrong with Veneleo?"

He glanced at the rim of the gully. "He's hit. We'll have to carry him out."

"Where is he?"

He untied the last knot. Emcasa and the Ersar-Aswero would be on them in seconds. If they went down the valley, toward Veneleo, they would collide with the Ersar-Aswero. Elinee didn't have a gun and according to his indicator he couldn't fire one more shot than he had to. They would have to run, not fight.

He started backing up the gully, away from the Ersar-Aswero. He waved his gun impatiently. "Come on. Hurry! I'll tell you later."

Chapter 14

Emcasa maneuvered into a position on a hill in the center of the valley and the Ersar-Aswero started driving them toward the automatic weapon. Every way they went a crossbow or a burst from Emcasa brought them to a halt. Emcasa commanded the valley and the slopes of the ridges and the *crar* still had enough warriors to patrol whatever the terrain hid from his view. Little by little the Ersar-Aswero pushed them toward the hill.

Veneleo's groans were unnerving. Every time he talked to them his whispers seemed noticeably weaker. They kept telling him they would soon be with him, but their voices betrayed their lack of confidence.

Crouching in a twisted jumble of rocks near the base of Emcasa's hill, Jenorden peered up the slope through a crack between two boulders. They had been driven here through a system of gullies and he was certain the Ersar-Aswero were now creeping toward them through those same gullies. Uphill was the only direction open to them, but if he tried to rush it his shield would collapse long before he reached the top. There was enough cover—a gully, rocks, an overhang at the bottom—so that he could hope to get part way up. But the final rush would kill him.

"Jenorden! Elinee!" From the top of the hill Emcasa blared at them with all the power of the loudspeaker in his space suit. "We have you surrounded. Don't make us take you by force. We might kill you in the struggle. I don't want to kill you! Surrender! I beg you to surrender. Your position is hopeless."

Jenorden picked up a crossbow bolt he had plucked from the dirt the last time an Ersar-Aswero had shot at them. A plan had been taking shape in his mind since he had first realized they couldn't break through the Ersar-Aswero ring.

"We have to get rid of Emcasa," he said. "Eliminate that gun and the Ersar-Aswero will be reduced to something we can handle."

She glanced at the bolt. "With that? And one of us stays here with the gun?" She couldn't conceal her distaste.

He nodded. She avoided his eyes and then she looked at him with a face full of sympathy. He unsnapped his pistol from the wires which connected it to his converter and she took it and hooked it to her own converter.

He put his hand on her shoulder and they came together and embraced. His lips tingled to kiss her. He wanted to return to the ship and satiate himself with her.

Elinee felt the change in the way he held her. She stepped back and their eyes said more than any touch could.

He looked away, returning to reality as he automatically checked the approaches the Ersar-Aswero might use any moment. The entire profound, intense exchange had lasted only a few seconds.

What difference did it make? His shoulders drooped and the sudden unexpected rush of passion drained from his body. His awakening emotions only made him more aware of the truth that violence and death of the last months had impressed on his consciousness. He was about to die. Even if he lived, it would only be to die some other day.

He had known that when he left Earth, but he had only known it with his brain. Now he knew it with his emotions. He had gone forth, hungry and curious, to possess the stars, and he had learned the only truth the stars could teach.

Even as he began to desire Elinee, he knew he would never again desire anything very much. It would always be like this. The desire would begin to stir and then his knowledge would deaden it. And in his world, a world without necessity, a man was only as alive as his desires.

Elinee responded to the change in his mood. "Jenorden..."

"Do you want to live, Elinee?"

"Don't you?"

"I'll have to kill him."

"He's almost our own kind."

His fingers gripped the iron bolt. He turned up the loudspeaker on his suit.

"Emcasa!"

"Are you ready to surrender, Jenorden?"

"Let us go free. I don't want to kill you."

"I don't want to kill you!"

"Then let us go free."

"If you want to live throw out your weapons and come out in the open." He sounded excited. He probably thought they were ready to give in.

"I'm going to kill you," Jenorden yelled. "Don't make me kill you."

"Don't threaten me! I can't be threatened!"

Jenorden turned to Elinee. "You know what to do." His voice sounded listless. "Don't let the Ersar-Aswero get you while you're covering me." He gestured with the bolt. "Put two shells on top of the hill."

She raised the pistol and shot between the crack. Two explosions raised the dirt just below Emcasa's position, and the wind blew the dust up the slope and obscured the hilltop.

He sprinted across the open ground between the rocks and the bottom of the hill. Emcasa's weapon chattered, firing blindly through the dust and the smoke. He reached the overhang at the base of the hill. Keeping his balance by digging his hands into the flat face of the overhang, he moved around the hill toward a gully.

He dropped into the gully. Holding the savage weapon in his hand, he crawled up the hill. The gully narrowed and he climbed out of it behind a twisted rock. He took his bearings and then he broke from cover and ran toward another rock. Surprised, Emcasa reacted too late and fired a short, angry burst.

"Go back, Jenorden! Surrender! You can't fight me unarmed."

He crept up the hillside from cover to cover until he reached a protecting rock face just below the final coverless expanse of hill. He was reasonably certain Emcasa didn't know exactly where he was. There had been no firing the last time he broke from hiding. He stared bleakly at the sharpened metal and signaled Elinee with his hand.

She fired six shots, one after the other. A barrage tore up the hillside. He counted the explosions. As soon as number six hit, he stood up and charged through the dust.

The automatic weapon swept the hillside. Again the wind blew the dust upward and covered the hilltop with a thick cloud. Guessing which direction Emcasa was facing from the sound of the gunfire, Jenorden circled left and leaped through the dust.

Emcasa was firing from a hollow he had dug in the hilltop. He tried to roll onto his back and bring the gun around and Jenorden fell on him, pushing the gun away with his free hand. Through their dust streaked suits they glared at each other like animals. Emcasa saw the bolt and a horrible sound, amplified by the loudspeaker, burst from his mouth. He grabbed Jenorden's forearm and the two of them struggled and kicked in the dirt. Jenorden fought Emcasa's legs with his own longer legs. His free hand held Emcasa's right arm pinned to the ground. He jerked his right arm up, pulling it free of Emcasa's grip.

"Surrender! Surrender!" He was pleading.

Emcasa grabbed his forearm again. His short legs thrashed as he tried to break the grip of the stronger, heavier human. Jenorden forced the point toward the breast of his suit.

"Surrender!"

"Murderer! Savage!"

"Don't make me kill you."

Emcasa answered with an insult. Jerking the hand which was pinned to the ground, he tried to pull Jenorden off balance. Jenorden shifted his weight and pressed the point a little closer.

"You're beaten. You can't survive. Surrender."

Emcasa glared at him. The point hovered an inch above the thick material of the space suit. Revolted by the savagery of the weapon, he hesitated. His own muscles would drive the weapon through flesh and bone. He would have to keep pushing even after Emcasa's face registered the first shock and pain.

He looked away from Emcasa's face and saw the gun lying just beyond his reach. He jumped up. Dropping the bolt, he picked up the gun and leaped backward. Emcasa came up roaring with fight. Jenorden pointed the gun at him and he froze.

"Raise your arms," Jenorden panted. "I couldn't use the bolt, but

I can use this."

Emcasa lowered his head. Inside the helmet his horns pointed at Jenorden's chest.

"Raise your arms," Jenorden repeated.

Emcasa raised his arms. "You're still surrounded. You aren't out of here yet."

Three explosions, soft, mushy sounds borne on the wind, went off down below. Jenorden glanced down the hill. Emcasa bent and hurled his heavily encumbered body at Jenorden's knees.

The automatic weapon hammered against Jenorden's hands. Bullets tore up the back of Emcasa's helmet. The gun climbed and more bullets pierced Emcasa's back and legs.

Jenorden stared at the body. Crouching, he searched for some sign of life.

He looked up. "Did you like that?" he asked the Borg. "Did you learn anything? Did it amuse you?"

Another explosion made him stand up. Elinee was running up the hill with the Ersar-Aswero bounding after her. Two armored bodies were sprawled near the jumble of rocks.

He raised the automatic weapon to his shoulder. He didn't shoot to kill, but the bullets swept the hillside and the Ersar-Aswero bounded for cover. He followed them with short, choppy bursts. Elinee struggled up the hill and threw herself flat in the hollow.

She stared at the body. "I killed him," Jenorden said.

"At least you did it with the gun."

"He wouldn't surrender."

She fired down the hillside. Realizing he was exposed to the Ersar-Aswero crossbows, he crouched beside her.

"Don't give in now," she said. "We still have to help Veneleo. I think I know how you feel, but try to force yourself." She frowned. "We haven't heard from him in a long time."

"I'm here," Veneleo whispered. "I've had my transmitter turned off."

"Emcasa's dead," Elinee said. "Now it's just us and the Ersar-Aswero. Can you sent up a flare?"

"Not yet," Jenorden said. His voice sounded hoarse and listless but his brain was still functioning. "The Ersar-Aswero here probably don't know where he is either. I don't think they have radios. We'll send up a flare and you can guide us, Veneleo."

"You're still thinking," Veneleo said. "I'm glad it's you I'm with."

"If it weren't for me, you wouldn't be here."

"Is the pain any worse?" Elinee asked.

"I feel numb. I think I went over the pain threshold a while ago."

They sent up the flare and then they sneaked down the back of the hill and started working their way down the valley. They did as little shooting as they could. Jenorden carried the automatic weapon and some ammunition he had taken from Emcasa, but he only shot to frighten and, when he had to, to wound. Whenever they thought it was safe, they sent up another flare and Veneleo gave them a new fix on his position.

They had been in the dome a long time. To their eyes the twilight was now almost total darkness. About half the stars in the sky were already visible.

Veneleo was sprawled on a ledge near the bottom of a steep cliff. They reached him just before nightfall. They ran across the open with a flare from Veneleo's pistol lighting the ground, and behind them the Ersar-Aswero gave up the chase and took cover.

Veneleo collapsed as soon as they arrived. Elinee watched the open ground and Jenorden uncoiled the ultra-thin wire splint in his first-aid kit and used it to immobilize the broken leg as soon as contact with human body warmth hardened the metal. The bolts were still inside Veneleo's limbs, but the holes in his suit had sealed without a flaw and his indicators said the suit's antibiotic system was fighting off infection. If they could get him to the ship in a few hours, the hospital might not have to replace anything.

Jenorden studied their position. "We'll have to carry him and we can't do that and fight them at the same time."

"We can't leave," Elinee said, "and they can't get at us. Of course now that it's night..."

"Maybe I can reason with them." He turned up the volume of his loudspeaker. Again he struggled to express himself in a language he had studied very briefly. "Warriors of the Ersar-Aswero *crar*! You have fought well. You are brave and ruthless opponents. I apologize for my insult. If we weren't better armed then you, we'd be dead now. Look at the position here. We can't leave unless you let us. We have to carry our wounded friend. You, on the other hand, cannot attack us across the open ground. Why not let us go? Why continue a useless fight? Let us go now and we'll give medical aid to your wounded. We can save many who are now dying."

He waited. Far above him the wind howled along the face of the cliff. Veneleo groaned and moved his free hand fretfully toward his wounded forearm.

"Noble enemies! Honored warriors!" The voice came from their left. "Our *crar* is dead. You have destroyed our *crar*. The *crar* has died and you must die with it."

The words fell on his consciousness as if they were blows. "You'll all die! You'll die for nothing! Listen to reason!"

Only the wind answered him.

"I was afraid of that," Elinee said.

"Why don't the Borg stop this? How can they watch and let this happen? What kind of things are they?"

She put her hand on his shoulder. "Keep thinking, Jenorden. Don't fall apart. I need you. As far as the Ersar-Aswero are concerned, they're already dead. When we killed so many of their *crar*, it was as if we'd mortally wounded an individual. They want to die. Dying honorably is all they have left. We aren't killing thirty of them to save three of us — we're killing one individual."

He took Veneleo's pistol and attached it to his converter. He stood up and once again he turned up the volume of his loudspeaker.

"Warriors of the Ersar-Aswero *crar*! Attack with all your skill and courage. Do your best. If we live, your *crar* will be a legend on every world in the galaxy. Do your best. We are not afraid." He crouched and his voice dropped to a whisper. "We are not afraid…"

Chapter 15

Sometimes they came alone, creeping through the dark and landing on the ledge with their iron swords swinging. Sometimes they came by twos and threes and Jenorden and Elinee shot them under the light of the flares. Every time Jenorden pulled a trigger, his rage swelled. Every time an Ersar-Aswero died, something in him died. They had robbed him of every passion except anger. He was a killer animal standing alone beneath the stars and the only claim to humanity he still possessed was his outrage against the beings who had done this to him. Take that away and he would be a *thing*, too.

In the morning they looked across a battleground strewn with armored corpses. The *crar* was dead.

He hurled his pistol across the field. He kicked a flock of expended cartridges off the ledge and then he picked up Emcasa's automatic weapon and swung it against the face of the cliff.

"Jenorden!"

Chips of rock spattered on his suit. Little by little the tough metal bent. The firing mechanism sprang apart and he kicked it off the ledge. It bounced and slid into a gully and he lowered his eyes and saw the dead Ersar-Aswero. He moaned and covered his face with his hands.

"Veneleo," Elinee said. "We have to get Veneleo to the hospital."

He wasn't insane. His life seemed like a prison in which he would be tortured by knowledge until he died; his disgust with himself and with a universe where such things could happen was a passion he had to release; but he wasn't insane. He knew what he was supposed to do and he could still go through the motions.

He uncovered his eyes. He looked angry and defeated at the same time. Elinee looked away from him and blanked her face.

They bent over Veneleo, who was mumbling in his sleep. Jenorden picked up his shoulders and Elinee picked up his boots. It wasn't the best way to carry him, but they didn't have a stretcher and the hospital would repair any damage they did. Silently they lugged their burden across the dark landscape. They were both physically exhausted. They had to stop and rest every few minutes.

"Is this how our ancestors lived?" Elinee asked. "I thought I understood history, but now I wonder how they managed to get so far. How did they keep their desire to do anything?"

When they arrived at the ship a wheeled stretcher was waiting in the airlock. He helped Elinee and Roseka transfer Veneleo, and then he watched the stretcher roll away from the airlock with the two women walking beside it. Pushing himself back into the zero gravity of the orbiting vehicle, he floated through the cabin to the pilot seat.

Once again he trudged across the wasteland from the vehicle to the Borg dome. This time the Borg were already waiting for him. There seemed to be more of them than usual and they were spread out along the curve of the dome at several levels.

He glared upward at the black shapes and the shifting gases.

"Have you counted the dead in that dome? What kind of beasts are you? You made this world. You made it and you brought us all here and then you let that slaughter happen. Did you like it? Did you learn anything?"

"Jenorden, Jenorden. Control yourself. We know how you feel. We're as miserable as you are."

"If you watched that and didn't stop it, you aren't even alive. You're dead and you're trying to kill everything else in the universe."

"We watched it all and we suffered. We're suffering now. If we could have stopped it, we would have. Believe us — we wanted to stop it."

"Then why didn't you?"

"We almost did. It's been a long time since we were that tempted."

"Why didn't you? Justify yourselves! Answer me!"

"You didn't have to leave your dome. We didn't make you leave your dome."

"If you don't justify now what you're doing, I'll leave this world today and I'll spend the rest of my life telling the galaxy to shun you. I'll tell them everything that's happened here. I'll tell them of all the brave, intelligent beings who died because of your folly. Everywhere you send the Ivel, they'll be met with suspicion and hatred. As far as I'm concerned, you're some kind of disease trying to spread itself through the galaxy."

"You'll ruin everything we're trying to do. You don't know what you're doing."

"What you're trying to do has already ruined too many good lives. Tell me why every being in the galaxy shouldn't be warned to avoid you. Tell me something that outweighs all the evidence I can give them."

"We want to. We want to tell you everything. Go back to your dome, follow the lectures, and you'll understand. Can't you be patient?"

"As patient as Rotrudo? How many years will it take? Ten? Fifty? Why should I waste my life span?"

"You have to be prepared. What we're doing... if we told you now, you wouldn't understand. You probably couldn't accept it. It might even disgust you."

"I'll take the risk. What have I got to lose?"

There was a long silence. Random noise crackled on the loudspeaker. He stared at them and tried to discover some clue to what they were doing, but they remained featureless and motionless as ever.

"You've given us no choice," the loudspeaker said. "You'll ruin everything. We have to tell you."

Chapter 16

The ship drifted away from the Borg sun. The metal shutters slid across the windows and the four humans strolled out of the control room and selected drinks and food from the buffet.

They were full of emotion but they savored the food without speaking. No words could possibly express what they were feeling. This was a day they had struggled toward for many years. Even their movements and the swift looks they exchanged revealed only a part of their tension and their buoyant excitement.

Jenorden walked to the pool, where his instrument was lying in the bottom of a chair. His emotions were too big to hold. He had to have music. Putting down his glass, he sat down and started a song they all knew. Elinee and Roseka picked up first and second violins and Veneleo put a metal wind instrument to his lips.

The music got louder and wilder. Roseka put down her instrument and started dancing. Veneleo and Elinee clapped their hands and shouted. Jenorden strummed and bowed as loud as he could and Roseka's soft hips and driving legs responded as if the music were originating inside her own nervous system. She danced with the uninhibited grace of a being that wasn't ashamed of anything it felt.

Veneleo stepped forward and started dancing with her. Soon they were all dancing, sometimes one of them alone, sometimes three of them and one playing, sometimes all of them together with no accompaniment except their own voices. The light years were speeding by, and they knew it, and they knew dangers and unknown terrors waited for them ahead, but they were riding to their fate with live bodies and full hearts.

"Attention," the computer said. "Attention. We are approaching our destination."

The shutters slid back. They returned to the control room and Veneleo gave the computer instructions. The instrument board lit up. Screens began projecting views of the ocean-covered world below. Detector beams probed down through the atmosphere and under the turbulent surface of the ocean. Traversing an orbit which crossed the equator at a forty-five degree angle, they reconnoitered the planet.

The results were as bad as they had feared. The Horta had established complete control over the Sordini and every other native life form. Under the paranoid repressions of the invaders, the drives and hungers of an entire world were clamoring for release. They were about to descend on a planet crawling with madness.

They stood up. For a moment they joined hands in a ring. Jenorden looked at them, his friends, his comrades, and he swelled with joy. Where in all the universe would he discover finer creatures? Who could have known that life could achieve so much? Whatever happened to them down below, no one here would falter. They would overcome the sickness of the Horta, or they would die in the attempt.

They went to the airlock and put on their suits. One by one they boarded the orbit-to-ground vehicle. Jenorden took the controls and the others strapped themselves into the passenger seats.

They were unarmed. They didn't even have their shields. When they landed on the suffering world below and opened their minds to the Horta, their only weapons would be what they were and the way their differing personalities were organized. They were not the same people they had been when they had first landed on this world, and they were now organized in the same way the Borg were organized, and for the same purpose. No other race in this galaxy had ever been organized for that purpose. In this vast, slowly revolving island of stars, they were something new. They were probably the next step in the evolution of their species.

Jenorden manipulated the controls. Behind him Elinee started a song they had selected before they left the Borg world. The rockets flared into life and they drifted away from the ship. Singing with all the power of their strong, almost gay, voices, they began their descent.

The Borg were from another galaxy. They had arrived in this galaxy less than a century before the four human wanderers had landed on their planet-ship. Sometime during the four million years of their history, they had reached the limit of their development, they had become all they were capable of being, and they had acquired a new need, a passion which had sent groups of them across the widest gulfs in the universe. They had stopped seeking power and knowledge and immortality and they had found themselves driven by an emotion grander than any passion any human had ever known—a passion for the development and fulfillment of all life. They could not keep what they had achieved to themselves. They thought of life springing into being all over the universe, races evolving which needed their knowledge, and even the gulfs between the galaxies couldn't hold them back. Where men and other intelligent life forms wandered the stars seeking what they could get, pleasures, and knowledge, and new powers, the Borg, having acquired all they were capable of absorbing, wandered the universe driven by an urgent need to give.

He had been stunned when he had first learned the immensity of life's potential. The Borg were not the ultimate in evolution. Indeed, on the cosmic scale their intelligence might be far below average. Even as he would seem like a god to the men of only three or four centuries ago, so his descendants would seem like gods to the Borg. But they would grow on what the Borg had given them, which was all the Borg asked, and when they reached their limit, they would do what the Borg had done. They would give all they had to other races, races which would eventually surpass them.

All life was growing. There was no limit to what life could be. Individuals and races had their limits, but life itself was unlimited, and every living creature could contribute to its growth. Individuals and races died and were forgotten, but what they had done and what they had been could never be extinguished, for it became part of the evolution of all life.

In all that infinity of possibilities, there was only one restriction. No race could know the potential of another race. Races could learn and they could borrow, but nothing of value could be forced on them. The older races could only offer and help. Hard as it sometimes was, they had to let the younger races make their mistakes. Force could destroy and subdue, but it could not develop.

The Borg had given him a vision of the universe men might not have achieved for millennia, if ever. It was a vision he had lived with for ten years now and it still excited and disturbed him. But it was no more disturbing than the moment when he had first heard the Borg confess their passion. If he lived a thousand years, as he might, he would never forget his surprise, even his horror and disgust, when he heard the soft Borg voices telling him their secret.

"Jenorden A'Ley, we love you."

The Making of *I Want the Stars*

by Tom Purdom

Doubling Up

In their biography *Tracy and Hepburn*, Garson Kanin and Ruth Gordon compare a career in the arts to a ride on a roller coaster. Every up is followed by a down, every down by an up. The winners are the people who hang on.

In August of 1963, my writing career was going through a down. I had sold two stories since I had been drafted in July 1959. I had spent most of the last four years trying to sell a novel and none of my attempts had succeeded.

I started working on novels when I was in the army. In those days most SF novels were published as paperback originals and you normally sold a novel by circulating three sample chapters and an extensive outline of the rest of the book.

My first attempt was a novel version of my *Galaxy* novelette "Sordman the Protector." I called it *I Feel My Power Flowing* and it took Sordman from his discovery that he had psi powers through the struggles and character development that produced the hero of the novelette. It didn't sell, but Scott Meredith passed me some encouraging words from Damon Knight, who was doing some editing for a paperback publisher. Damon had rejected the package with the comment that "This is a writer to watch." Damon was one of the best short story writers in the field, a demanding critic, and an editor who was putting together a long string of anthologies.

I wrote at least two other sample chapter and outline packages, plus some short fiction that didn't sell. Then sometime in 1962, I decided to write a contemporary novel about the romances of young people living in center city Philadelphia. I wrote the entire novel and put it through two or three drafts in about nine months, finishing sometime in May or June 1963.

About two weeks after I finished it, I received a phone call from Terry Carr, who was handling my stuff at the Scott Meredith Literary Agency. Terry was a popular figure in the science fiction world. He had become a well-known fan while he was a teenager in California and his first short story sales had made him a highly visible young writer. He had started working for Scott Meredith after he moved to New York. Later, like a lot of Scott Meredith protégés, he transferred to the editorial side and became a noted book and anthology editor.

Terry had to tell me the agency didn't think the book was saleable. He was sorry but they were returning the manuscript. It was one of the gloomiest conversations I've ever had—just as gloomy for Terry, I think, as it was for me.

In February of that year, Sara had suffered a miscarriage. She had quit her job with the Presbyterian Board so we could have a child and we had both been building up all the emotions and anticipations that precede childbirth. Then, without warning, the whole process came to a halt.

The miscarriage was only the beginning of a tense period. A few days after it happened, Sara broke out with chickenpox. She had never had chickenpox when she was a child. She had apparently picked it up from a boy who lived on the first floor of the center city walkup apartment building we were living in. The chicken pox had probably triggered the miscarriage.

The chicken pox was followed by an incident Sara wanted to ignore—a sharp momentary pain in one of her eyes. I insisted she go to our eye doctor and she gave in—a decision that had a huge effect on the future of our life together. The disturbances in her system had activated an autoimmune response. Her immune system was attacking her eyes. If she had visited the eye doctor a few days later, she would probably have gone blind.

As it was, the doctor couldn't guarantee he could save her vision. She had to take cortisone for six weeks and hope the treatment would work. Once every week for six weeks, she trekked to the doctor's office and he looked for indications the condition was getting worse. Once every week for six weeks, I waited for my wife to call me at the office and tell me she wasn't going blind.

In May of 1963, a little after we had weathered Sara's eye crisis, we made a major change in our lifestyle. I stopped working full-time at my job as an airline reservation clerk and started working part-time.

We had gotten married in November of 1960, while I was still in the army. I got out of the army in July, 1961 and returned to the kind of work schedule I had been maintaining before I got drafted. I worked forty hours a week at the airlines, on rotating shifts, and wrote two hours every day, including my days off.

At some point I noticed that the reservations staff included part timers. I started thinking about part-time work and the idea became more and more attractive. It seemed to me my life was out of proportion. Writing was supposed to be my primary occupation but I was spending forty hours a week earning a living and only fourteen writing. My working life looked like a giant rocket with a tiny payload.

I discussed the matter with Sara and we worked out a budget. I broached the idea to my employers and we negotiated a schedule. I would work 9-2 at the airlines, Monday through Friday. Then I would eat lunch at home with Sara and write four hours every afternoon, plus four hours on Saturday morning. The airline liked that schedule because it meant they would only have to carry me on the payroll during some of their peak hours. Sara liked it, she said, because it meant her husband wouldn't disappear into his workroom for two hours every evening. We would have to live on a tighter budget but with luck I might make up the difference by writing more.

So now it was August. Sara could still see, my attempt to write a serious contemporary novel had failed, and our income was thirty-five percent smaller than it had been in May.

My novel projects had all been fairly ambitious efforts like *I Feel My Power Flowing*. I decided it was time I took two steps backward and tried something with guaranteed commercial potential. I decided I would aim for the Ace Double market.

Ace Doubles were paperback originals. Each Ace Double contained two novels, bound back to back, with a different cover on each side of the book. Ace Books paid the lowest advances in the field — a thousand dollars for each half of a double — and they specialized in the kind of stories science fiction fans referred to as "space opera." Ace Doubles were essentially the paperback successors to pulp magazines like *Planet Stories* and *Startling Stories* — magazines that had mostly carried adventure stories set in interplanetary and interstellar futures.

Like the pulps, Ace was a good market for hack writers — for people who could write very fast to minimum standards. If you could sell several novels a year to publishers like Ace, you could make a comfortable living, in the same way you could make a living churning out a story a week for the pulps in the 30s and 40s.

But there was more to it than that. Like the pulps, Ace also provided a market for other kinds of work. In the late 40s, at the end of the pulp era in science fiction, Ray Bradbury had sold much of his early work to the space opera markets. Most of the stories that eventually became part of *The Martian Chronicles*, and transformed him into a writer of international stature, were originally published in low paying pulps like *Startling* and *Thrilling Wonder*. At the beginning of the paperback era, in the same way, Philip K. Dick sold most of his work to Ace. Dick has become a cult literary figure over the last thirty years, but many of his novels started life as Ace Doubles.

The Ace Double format had the great virtue, in addition, that it could accommodate science fiction that didn't meet the length requirements for stand-alone novels. One of the classics of the early 60s, Jack Vance's *The Dragon Masters*, was a long novella. I read it when it first appeared in *Galaxy* and Ace published it as half of a double.

Last — and most important from my viewpoint — Ace was a good beginner's market. Samuel R. Delany and Ursula K. Le Guin both began their novel careers writing Ace Doubles. For most of us, Le Guin's first novel was *The Left Hand of Darkness*, which Terry Carr published as part of the Ace Special series he started after he left Scott Meredith and joined Ace. But Le Guin actually wrote three Ace books, two of them Doubles, before she wrote the novel that made her a major figure in the science fiction cosmos.

Ace was an attractive beginner's market because you just had to satisfy two requirements. You had to create a good action-adventure plot and you had to set it in a colorful, interesting future. The editor of Ace Books, Donald A. Wollheim, had been a science fiction fan since he had been a teenager in the 1930s. Don had been a member of the legendary fan group called The Futurians — a group whose membership had included future writers and editors such as Frederik Pohl, Damon Knight, and Isaac Asimov. Don grew up reading the science fiction pulps and he sometimes argued that science fiction was a branch of children's literature — a genre whose core audience consisted of bright teenage boys. He didn't object if your novel included things like good prose, interesting characters, and an original view of the future. But anybody who understood science fiction and its history could look at the covers of a rack full of Ace Doubles and know what the basic requirements were.

I once read an article by one of the leading British SF writers of the 60s, John Brunner, in which he said he liked to pick up a standard SF theme every now and then and see what he could do with it. I did something similar with my Ace Doubles. Each double was built around a standard science fiction situation. For my first try, I decided to write a story about humans exploring a mysterious planet.

I developed the idea using a technique I had encountered in an article by a mystery writer. You can create a mystery plot, the author pointed out, by asking yourself a series of questions. Who was murdered? Who did it? Why did they do it? Who are the other suspects? Who is the detective? Where does this take place?

It sounds like a mechanical process, but there's a catch. You must come up with the most interesting and original answers your brain can produce. People who dismiss this kind of thing as "formula writing" overlook an important fact. The so-called formula isn't a list of ingredients you can buy at your corner store. It's actually a set of *requirements*. The "formula" only provides you with the questions. You have to come up with the answers.

I don't know exactly when I started thinking about the mysterious planet idea. I do know when the whole book fell into place.

One night in August I went to the Gilded Cage (the coffeehouse where I met my wife) by myself. Sara was visiting her parents in Texas and I was on my own. I had thought I could hang around the Cage in the evenings while she was gone, but marriage had changed things. We no longer went to the Gilded Cage regularly. People we knew had drifted away and we hadn't linked up with most of the new regulars as they drifted in. We still had friends who frequented the Gilded Cage but none of them were there when I came through the door.

I sat down at a table by myself and did something I had never done before. I turned over one of the yellow sheets that contained the Gilded Cage menu and started writing notes on the back. Ideas started flowing through my head. The familiar dimly lit room became a remote background. By the time I finished filling the menu with notes I had worked out all the major events of the plot, including the ending. It took me less than an hour — possibly only twenty minutes.

A small group of humans land on a planet that confronts them with a big mystery. What kind of future society do they come from? Why are they there?

The standard answer to the first question would be some kind of galactic empire or interstellar federation. Hack writers could pull a prefabricated version of either one off the shelf. Better writers created something original and more interesting. James Schmitz's Agent of Vega stories took place in an interstellar federation but it was called a confederacy and it had its own unique politics and government. Poul Anderson's galactic empire was the final stage of a long historical process and he could set stories in intermediate stages such as the interstellar trading society of his Nicolas van Rijin stories. His Dominick Flandry adventure stories gain a special, ironic flavor because they take place in a *decadent* galactic empire — a dying society which his hedonistic hero defends on the grounds that it's preferable to more puritanical up-and-coming societies.

For my future society, I started with one of Arthur C. Clarke's pronouncements. Any interstellar travelers we encounter, Clarke had argued, are going to be peaceful. If they can build starships, they must have gone through technological stages that include nuclear weapons and other dangerous items. If they've survived the crises created by those developments, they've learned how to live together in peace.

I decided my future society would incorporate my vision of the kind of world we could create if we survived the nuclear crisis and our economic and technological progress continued at its current pace. The human life span has been extended to four hundred years and humans go through a forty-seven year educational process that guarantees they will be peaceful members of the human community. The society is so wealthy and technologically advanced that five young people in their first century of life can acquire a faster than light starship merely by requesting it. No one has to work or do anything else they don't want to do.

For my characters' motivation, I turned to an idea that had intrigued me ever since I read a novelette called "Brightside Crossing" by Allen Nourse, a writer who worked his way through the University of Pennsylvania Medical School writing dozens of science fiction stories, and eventually became a successful science writer. In all the science fiction stories I could remember, characters usually had military or economic motives for their adventures. "Brightside Crossing" was written at a time when we thought Mercury kept one side exposed to the sun and it tells the story of two men who attempt to traverse the entire "brightside" in tractors. The stunt has no practical value. They can't even claim they're researchers or explorers. They do it for the same reason people climb mountains or sail around the world alone—for the achievement itself and the emotional satisfaction it gives them.

My space travelers would wander the galaxy merely because they could do it. "They lived in the dawn of human freedom," I wrote at the end of the second chapter. "Masters of the star drive, citizens of a human community so wealthy it could satisfy every material desire without human labor" they "went where they wanted and did what they pleased. They followed their hearts and nothing else."

So what is the mystery that confronts them? What is the solution?

The plot I had developed at the Gilded Cage revolved around a mysterious super race called the Borg. My young adventurers get tired of touring worlds humans have already visited. They enter an unexplored star cluster and learn the Borg are offering to answer any question anyone asks. The Borg have occupied an uninhabited planet and dispatched emissaries to intelligent races throughout the cluster. Everyone is invited to visit the Borg planet. All questions will be answered. Their emissaries are even visiting races that haven't developed interstellar travel and offering to transport their representatives to the Borg planet.

To the humans this is a horrifying idea. Their species has just squeaked through a period in which it was almost destroyed by high-speed technological change. Humans have adopted the principle—a common one in the science fiction of the period—that it's criminal to introduce advanced ideas to less advanced species. The humans go to the Borg planet where representatives from a number of different species have been given habitats, and a series of violent episodes lead to the climactic moment when the hero, Jenorden A'Ley, confronts the Borg and learns their motive.

For the humans, the heart of the mystery is the motivation of the Borg. Why would anyone do such a thing? The solution was heavily influenced by a short story by one of the leading science fiction writers of the day, "Saucer of Loneliness" by Theodore Sturgeon. In Sturgeon's story, the main character asks why we always imagine superbeings will have super powers, such as super intelligence or super strength. Why can't they have super emotions? Such as super love? Or super loneliness?

The revelation of the Borg's purpose is combined with a cosmic vision that is related to Jenorden's main preoccupation. Jenorden is haunted by the contrast between his own limited consciousness and the immensity of a universe in which a single galaxy harbors thousands of intelligent species. It's a feeling many of us have when we contemplate the universe revealed to us by modern cosmology, but it is normally peripheral. For Jenorden, it is one of his primary motivators.

I had theorized that you could build characters by taking one of your minor emotions and making it the central emotion of a character's life. I believe this is the only time I've put that theory into practice.

There was an obvious conflict between the peaceful human society Jenorden and his friends came from and the fact that I was writing an Ace Double action story. I resolved this by assuming that my characters had a limited right to self-defense. Jenorden can fight back—and even kill — if he's attacked by one or two people. He might even kill a dozen attackers. But at some point beyond that — and not too far beyond that — he becomes emotionally incapable of killing.

Humans have developed this psychological inhibition — which is imbedded in their personalities by the long educational process imposed on them — as a defense against the possibilities created by nuclear weapons. They have eliminated their psychological ability to unleash weapons of mass destruction.

As I mentioned in the last chapter, "ticking time bombs" are an important aspect of plotting. You increase the pressure on your hero by adding an element that imposes a time limit. The psychological inhibition presented me with a time bomb that started ticking every time my characters became involved in an action scene. Sooner or later, at some unknown point, they were going to reach the limit of their capacity for violence. In one of my favorite scenes in the story, Jenorden is caught in a horrific fight. At the climax of the scene, he reaches his emotional limit and does something no action hero is supposed to do. He stops fighting and starts running.

I once wrote an unsuccessful story about a telepathic race called the Horta, after being impressed by a Poul Anderson story about the disadvantages of telepathy. Telepaths, I had decided, could easily slip into paranoia. They would be constantly receiving the thoughts and emotions of the people around them and some of the feelings they picked up would be feelings they were repressing. In their attempts to repress the forbidden thoughts, they might lash out at the sources and attempt to destroy them. The Horta were an entire race of paranoid telepaths.

During my reverie in the Gilded Cage, I had decided I couldn't start the book with my characters arriving on the mysterious planet. I needed a good action scene for an opening hook. I decided to resurrect the Horta.

The book begins with the humans strapped into an orbit-to-ground vehicle which is preparing to attack a Horta starship that is sitting on a small island on an alien planet. The Horta are the first telepaths any humans have encountered and they are enslaving the inhabitants of the planet, an amphibious race called the Sordini. Jenorden and his friends have decided to attack the Horta ship, and save the Sordini, in a spirit of youthful bravado.

The attack fails. The Horta enter their minds and turn their deepest feelings against them. They amplify Jenorden's cosmic angst and turn it into paralyzing despair. The humans resume their wanderings chastened by the experience and encounter the emissaries of the Borg.

I devised the scene to give the book a fast opening. My musings at the Gilded Cage eventually turned the clash with the Horta into a conclusion that gave the book an overall shape. The next to the last chapter ends with Jenorden demanding to know the Borg's purpose. When the last chapter opens, several years have passed and the humans are preparing to leave the Borg planet and take on the Horta armed with the psychological protection they have acquired from the Borg. The chapter then works backward through the Borg's vision of the cosmos to the final line of the book, the revelation Jenorden received when he demanded that the Borg explain themselves.

Star Trek fans will probably note that the Star Trek universe also includes two species named the Borg and the Horta. People have asked me about the coincidence but I have no idea how it happened.

The Borg received their name from one of the components of the hi-fi set we bought just after I got out of the army. Horta was derived from my memories of the Marlon Brando movie *Viva Zapata*, which included a Mexican dictator named General Huerta.

I started working on the book shortly after I sketched it in at the Gilded Cage. I finished the first three chapters and a long outline in October. The outline was about ten thousand words long. I had read an article in *Writer's Digest* which recommended detailed outlines that long. Nowadays you will generally be told an outline should run about six to twelve pages — and the closer to six the better.

Short outlines were pretty standard in 1963, too, according to what Terry Carr told me, but I found it easier to write long outlines. I wrote very detailed scenarios when I was planning a story, with completely choreographed fight scenes. I could put together a long outline by retyping the scenario and adding a little polishing. A short outline would have required more thought.

I got a letter from Terry about a week after I mailed him the package. He advised me he was sending it out to market and noted that it was "a strange book, Edmond Hamilton *cum* Theodore Sturgeon" — Edmond Hamilton being a legendary exponent of pulp space opera who was affectionately referred to as "World Wrecker Hamilton."

On August 28, 1963, I had interrupted work on the book to visit Washington, along with some 200,000 other people, and express my views on civil rights, racial integration, and related matters. It was the first March on Washington since the Depression and there was widespread fear it might lead to violence. It was so peaceful, in fact, that the minister at Sara's church took the first verse of Psalm 133 as his text when he discussed the March in his sermon the following Sunday: *Behold how good and how pleasant it is for brethren to dwell together in unity.*

I went to the March with my friend Jerry Dunwoody, an advertising man who played an important role in my writing career when he went into business on his own twenty years later. Sara stayed home because she was pregnant and we didn't want to run the risk she would have another miscarriage. At one point in our wanderings on the Mall, Jerry and I ran into Dick Eney, a prominent Washington science fiction fan. Dick was wearing the badge of the Hyborean Legion — the national organization for sword and sorcery fans named after the Hyborean Age, the mythical time in which a barbarian named Conan fought his way to the throne of the richest kingdom in his world. When I kidded Dick about the badge, he said he felt they should be represented, too.

Martin Luther King didn't know it, but a representative of the King of Aquilonia, Conan the Cimmerian, was standing in the audience when he made his famous "I have a dream" speech.

Sara's minister, Lacey Harwell, was a Southern liberal — a type of person who has always had a special place in my affections. Lacey was firmly opposed to racial segregation and all the attitudes that accompanied it, but he could never forget that the people on the other side were human beings, too. For someone like him, they could never be stereotyped racists or rednecks. They were the friends and relations he had grown up with.

The church was located in West Philadelphia, near the borderline between the University of Pennsylvania campus and the remains of a black neighborhood. In September, Lacey announced that the church was starting a remedial reading tutoring program. Everyone who participated in the March on Washington had been asked to pledge that they would do something for the cause when they returned home and Lacey's tutoring program seemed like a good way to fulfill that obligation. On a sunny Saturday in October, one week after I got Terry's letter, I attended a training session at the Bryn Mawr Presbyterian Church, in the Philadelphia suburbs. I got back to our apartment about three in the afternoon.

Sara was standing in the living room with a smile on her face when I opened the door. We had a cedar chest located where I could see it from the door and I could see an arrangement she had set out on top of it. My eyes took in three items laid out in a little overlapping stack—a manila envelope, a mimeographed document that was obviously a contract, and, on top of everything, one of the small manila note papers Scott Meredith employees used for stationery.

"Don bought the book," I said. And Sara nodded.

When I look back on that moment now, I'm aware of something I took for granted at the time. My first short story sale had left me feeling it was an unshareable experience. Most of the people you know will either overreact and be awed that you have entered the hallowed ranks of the published or wonder why you're making such a fuss over an acceptance from a publisher like Ace Books. Very few non-writers understand the concept of a beginner's market.

This time I didn't feel I was having an unshareable experience. This time I had a companion who knew precisely what it meant.

So now I had to write the rest of the book. The contract contained a deadline that gave me three months to finish the job, "time being of the essence."

It was an abnormally short deadline. The industry norm for a book was probably a full year, judging by the comments I received from one or two older writers.

Ace's payment schedule was another deviation from standard publishing practice. The standard contract paid half the advance on signing and half on completion. Ace authors received one third on signing, one third on completion, and the final third on publication. The three payments were calculated to the last penny.

Ace had deep roots in the heyday of the pulp magazines, when writers like Max Brand wrote whole novels in a weekend and the lower level magazines paid on publication, rather than on acceptance.

The impact of this real-life ticking time bomb was magnified by another opportunity that had come my way. Fredrik Pohl had added a new magazine, *Worlds of Tomorrow*, to the two magazines he was already editing, *Galaxy* and *If*. Fred had circulated a request for non-fiction pieces for the new magazine, Terry had sent me a copy, and I had suggested an article on the future of the city. Fred liked the idea and I now found myself committed to writing my first novel and my first magazine article with a ridiculously tight deadline looming over me. I had also agreed to devote one night a week to Lacey Harwell's tutoring program.

If I were writing the city article today, I would probably feel I had to conduct several interviews. For *Worlds of Tomorrow*, I based the piece on library research and my own thoughts on the future of the city. A friend who was a librarian at Drexel University searched their catalog and presented me with a stack of books that supported different viewpoints. I plowed through half a dozen and added a book I had been planning to read—Jane Jacob's *The Death and Life of Great American Cities*. The article became a survey which pitted Jane Jacob's enthusiasm for the dense, economically diversified big city—which I shared—against the sprawling, automobile oriented visions of thinkers like Frank Lloyd Wright.

I can't remember how long it took me to write the article, but I believe I did all the reading and mailed Terry a finished manuscript in about three weeks. Fred was the Principal Speaker at the Philadelphia Science Fiction Conference in November and he told me he was buying the article shortly after he arrived at the conference.

Like a lot of other science fiction writers, I discovered that I liked writing non-fiction. Non-fiction is a natural offshoot of a science fiction career. It's easier to write, it pays better, and the research that goes into many science fiction stories can be turned into magazine articles. During the next two years I wrote another article for Fred and solidified my credits as a beginning journalist by writing three articles for a highly satisfactory middle-level national market, the *Kiwanis* magazine.

Some writers have problems with the transition from the short story to the novel. My biggest problem was the need to write longer, more detailed scenes. In a short story, you can usually skip mundane details like entrances and exits and exchanges of greetings. In a novel, they're sometimes unavoidable. I kept running into passages in which I had to develop interesting ways to handle that kind of thing. The contract called for a 50,000 word book and I had some trouble stretching the story to that length — an ironic problem, as it turned out.

President Kennedy was assassinated while I was working on the book and his death affected the way I handled certain scenes. At one point in the story, one of the most likable alien characters is shot from ambush while she's riding in a vehicle. I had been treating the violence in the story in a somewhat detached manner, as an exercise in plotting. When I reached that scene a couple of weeks after the assassination, I found that I had to take the violence more seriously. The story acquired darker overtones. My characters' reactions became deeper and more realistic.

Terry had advised me I could finish the book a little late, under the circumstances, but I believe I sent him the manuscript on time. It was, at most, just one or two days late.

Would Don like the book? Would I receive my second check? Had I actually succeeded in selling my first novel?

Yes, but.

Don liked the book, Terry informed me, but he wanted me to cut it by fifteen percent.

It was a particularly annoying request because I had struggled to get the book up to the length called for in the contract. Now, the editor was asking me to undo the very thing he had asked me to do when he had filled in the blanks in the contract form.

It wasn't going to be an easy job either. Terry and I both agreed I couldn't solve the problem by eliminating one or two episodes. The manuscript would have to be cut almost page by page, one or two sentences per page.

A cut like that would also call for some rewriting. You can't cut most manuscripts merely by eliminating words. In a lot of cases, you have to bridge the gap with new words.

Nowadays cutting is almost fun. You can hop around the manuscript on your computer screen and cut and rewrite anything that catches your attention. You can even check the word count now and then and stop cutting when your word processor returns the winning number. You can click Print when you're finished and watch your printer churn out a clean fifty thousand word manuscript in half an hour.

In the glorious days of the typewriter era — the days when writers had to have stamina and character and iron willed determination — extensive cutting was a much more laborious process. Words and sentences had to be lined out by hand. Pages had to be retyped. I had to keep a running total of the number of words cut on a scrap of paper.

I have no memory of the time I spent doing the cutting. I just know it got done. The revised manuscript went back to Ace and Terry eventually sent me my second check.

A couple of years after this incident, I mentioned it again when I was talking to Terry. I still couldn't understand why it had been necessary.

The two halves of an Ace double were supposed to total ninety thousand words, Terry told me. Don had ordered two fifty thousand word books.

I had called the book *I Want the Stars* — a reference to the cosmic hunger that drove Jenorden A'Ley. It was an awkward title, since the book wasn't written in the first person, but I had slapped it on when I started my initial planning and it had still been there when I mailed in the final manuscript. Don Wollheim frequently changed titles for commercial reasons, but my creation was still operating under its original name when Terry sent me a copy of the Ace flyer that advised distributors they would soon be receiving Ace Double F 289.

We had several paperback bookstores in center city Philadelphia in those days but none of them carried Ace Doubles. I had noted that the newsstand in the Greyhound bus station a few blocks from our apartment did sell Ace products and I trotted down there soon after the publication date listed in the flyer. And there it was — complete with the cover by Ed Emshwiller illustrated in the flyer.

People often ask how you feel when you first see a book with your name on it. I can remember three emotions.

Many science fiction readers were put off by the pulpy atmosphere that surrounded Ace but I actually liked it. I liked knowing my book would be sold in bus stations and drug stores. It took me back to the childhood days when I bought comic books and magazines like *Model Airplane News* at outlets like dime stores and outdoor magazine stands.

I can also remember feeling a peculiarly eerie sensation when I looked at the illustration in the flyer and saw the book on the newsstand. When a story appears in a magazine, you're part of a collective effort. You're one more name on a contents page. With a book, your name is the only name.

Other than that, I mostly felt relieved. I had struggled past one more checkpoint. There had been times during the last couple of years when I had felt like I was hanging from a cliff by my fingers. Now I felt like I was trudging up a steep slope.

Don Wollheim had discussed his publishing policies during a talk he gave at a Philadelphia Science Fiction Conference. He printed up one hundred thousand copies of each Ace Double, he said, and planned on selling seventy thousand. Some books reached that goal in six months, some took five years. He kept sending them back out until the sales figures hit the target.

I Want the Stars was paired with *Demon's World* by Kenneth Bulmer, a British author who was an Ace regular (which may explain why I got to be the guy who did the cutting). According to my royalty statements, the double was published July 20, 1964. By June 30, 1965, it had sold 65,300 copies. It passed the 70,000 mark by June 30, 1967 and it ultimately sold over 74,000 copies.

The standard book publishing contract gave US publishers the right to sell copies in the United States and its possessions, Canada, and the Philippines. British rights were a separate right which could be sold to a British publisher for an additional advance. Ace bought worldwide English language rights. That would normally be considered a no-no but it seemed reasonable to me, since airports were a major Ace outlet.

One of my close friends in the airline office actually saw the book on the airport racks when she got off a plane in Bangkok. We had a little fun playing around with the possibility she could have boosted my career by sending Ace a fan letter from Thailand. If she had, we decided, she would have told them it was a great book but it should have been fifteen percent longer.

Normally a first novel would be dedicated to the author's spouse. Sara and I both agreed that *I Want the Stars* should be dedicated to our friend Will Jenkins, who had been the best man at our wedding. Will had been hit with a stroke a few months before I went in the Army and we felt there was a real possibility he might die before I put a second book on the stands.

The first time I saw Will, he was opening the 1955 Philadelphia Science Fiction Conference. He introduced himself by noting that he was "the wrong Will Jenkins" — a reference to the fact that Will F. Jenkins was the real name of Murray Leinster, who had been one of the best known writers in the field for a couple of decades.

Will earned his living working as a clerk for the Baltimore and Ohio Railroad. He had never been to college but he was one of the best-read people I've ever met. He could talk about a pulp writer like Frederick Faust — who wrote under the name Max Brand — and switch without a pause to comments on the time he saw Laurence Olivier do *Oedipus Rex*. Like many of us in those days, he was especially fond of Hemingway's work.

He was one of the three close male friends I've had in my life. He was a thin, slightly awkward guy who wore glasses and possessed some of the reticent likeability Henry Fonda displayed on the screen. Sara and I accumulated a wonderful group of friends from the Philadelphia Science Fiction Society, the Gilded Cage, and the other focal points of our life in center city, and Will's wry, good-natured sense of humor made him one of the funniest people in a group that did a lot of laughing. He could even keep a bunch of people laughing while he showed off his slides of his trip to Disneyland, which he visited shortly after Walt Disney opened his Anaheim Utopia. Will's stroke had been my first confrontation with medical calamity. I was only twenty-two when it happened and I had never lost anyone.

When I went to see Will in the hospital a few days after the stroke, his mouth was twisted to one side, and his right arm was draped limply across the sheets. I found myself trapped in a common dilemma. Should I look at his distorted face and give him the impression I was staring? Should I avert my eyes and make him think he looked so bad I couldn't look at him?

Will was bantering with the other people who were there, in spite of the trouble he had talking, but he noticed my problem. He reached up with his good hand and ran it across his mouth.

"Lon Chaney did this bit in *The Mummy's Curse*," Will joked.

It was one of the most gallant things I've ever seen someone do — an example that has guided me ever since.

Will recovered most of the use of his arm. He was actually driving his little red MG sports car when he arrived at our wedding in November of 1960. Our son Christopher was born in April of 1964 and we got to share the birth and Christopher's first months with him. In July, I gave him a copy of the book with the dedication "For Will Jenkins of Philadelphia" — a phrasing I had chosen so it would be clear I wasn't dedicating the book to Murray Leinster. In October, I got a phone call telling me he had died suddenly of a massive heart attack.

When people ask me to autograph *I Want the Stars*, I sometimes write a famous line from *The Old Man and the Sea* under the dedication. "Man was not meant for defeat," the quote goes. "Man can be destroyed but not defeated."

Adapted from Installment Eight of "WHEN I WAS WRITING: A Literary Memoir" — the rest can be found at https://www.philart.net/tompurdom/wiwfour.htm.

About the Author

Thomas Edward Purdom (born 1936) is an American writer best known for science fiction and nonfiction. His story *Fossil Games* was a nominee for the Hugo Award for Best Novelette in 2000. He has also done music criticism since 1988. His works have been translated into German, Chinese, Burmese, Russian, and Czech. He lives in Philadelphia

His first short story, "Grieve for a Man," appeared in the August, 1957 *Fantastic Universe*, Hans Stefan Santesson, Editor. (Tom says: "Always mention the name of the first editor who had the good taste to actually pay you money for something you wrote.") Since then, his short stories and novelettes have appeared in *Asimov's*, *Analog*, *The Magazine of Fantasy and Science Fiction*, *Galaxy*, *Amazing*, other SF magazines, and various anthologies. Since 1988, he's been writing SF novelettes which have mostly appeared in *Asimov's*. His novels have appeared under the Ace imprint and the Berkley imprint.

He has edited one anthology, *Adventures in Discovery* (Doubleday, 1969), a collection of specially commissioned articles on science by Asimov, Silverberg, Anderson, and other leading science fiction writers of the time.

About the Publisher

Founded in 2019 by Galactic Journey's Gideon Marcus, Journey Press publishes the best science fiction, current and classic, with an emphasis on the unusual, the diverse, and stories of hope.

Also available from Journey Press:

Rediscovery
Science Fiction by Women (1958-1963)

The Silver Age of Science Fiction saw a wealth of compelling speculative tales — and women authors wrote some of the best of the best. Yet the stories of this era, especially those by women, have been largely unreprinted, unrepresented, and unremembered.

Until now.

Kitra by Gideon Marcus
A YA Space Adventure

Stranded in space: no fuel, no way home... and no one coming to help!

Nineteen-year-old Kitra Yilmaz dreams of traveling the galaxy like her Ambassador mother. But soaring in her glider is the closest she can get to touching the stars — until she stakes her inheritance on a salvage Navy spaceship.

THE
TWILIGHT
ZONE

DO YOU WANT TO
TRAVEL BACK
IN TIME?

WWW.GALACTICJOURNEY.ORG

the
AMAZING
SPIDER

THE
FANTASTIC
THINK I'M TR
BUT THEY
SUSPECT
REAL POW

ADDED ATTRACTION: SPIDE
CHAMELEO

HOME
by
McKENNA
THE SAND PEBBLES
LEIBER
RRY HARRISON